Donald Grant Mitchell

About old Story-Tellers

Donald Grant Mitchell

About old Story-Tellers

ISBN/EAN: 9783337367169

Printed in Europe, USA, Canada, Australia, Japan

Cover: Foto ©Andreas Hilbeck / pixelio.de

More available books at **www.hansebooks.com**

ABOUT
OLD STORY-TELLERS

OF HOW
AND WHEN THEY LIVED

AND

WHAT STORIES THEY TOLD

BY

DONALD G. MITCHELL

AUTHOR OF "REVERIES OF A BACHELOR," "MY FARM
OF EDGEWOOD," ETC., ETC.

NEW YORK
CHARLES SCRIBNER'S SONS
1898

TO THE SMALL COMPANY

AT EDGEWOOD,

AND TO THE LARGER COMPANY

WHOM THEY MEET

ONCE A MONTH

OVER THE PLEASANT PAGES OF "ST. NICHOLAS."

THIS LITTLE BOOK

IS AFFECTIONATELY DEDICATED

BY THEIR EARNEST WELL-WISHER,

D. G. M.

PREFACE.

9632

For the Grown-up People.

I MAKE no doubt that elderly people will browse at this booklet, in the shops, if no-where else ; testing what flavor it may have, and if it will be safe reading for Ned, or Tom, or Bell, or such other son or grandchild as may be pull-ing at old heart-strings for some token of kindly feeling, to mark the holidays.

For all such gracious elderly ones, I shall say a frank word here at the beginning about the pur-port of the book, and of the reasons why it has taken the shape it has, and of what good I hope it may do to the youngsters who thumb its pages and study its pictures.

In the matter of books, as in the world, I believe in old friends, and don't think they should be laid away upon the shelf without good cause; and age is hardly cause enough.

In short, I must confess a lurking fondness for those good old-fashioned stories which were current forty years ago, — and some of them maybe a hundred years ago, — written in good straightforward English, with good straightforward intent. I cannot get over or outlive the zest with which I first pored over the story of "Lazy Lawrence," or listened to it, or to that other of "Barring Out," intoned by lips on whose utterance I hung entranced. And if Miss Edgeworth won such yearning, what is to be said of "Robinson Crusoe," — of "Gulliver," — of "The Vicar of Wakefield?" Are these outlived? — or "The Arabian Nights," or Grimm's Stories, or John Bunyan's "Pilgrim"?

In my own household at least, as the evenings have grown long in winter, and the fire-play has thrown its gleams over wall and floor, I have sought to keep alive a regard for those old-new books; and have endeavored to kindle and fasten interest in them, by talk of their authors, and of the times in which they lived, and of the circumstances under which they wrote, — so that the

stories should be planted in the minds of the
young people — not as isolated bits of fancy having no historic surroundings, but as growing out
of definite epochs, and taking color from them,
and in their way illustrating them. And I have
sought by such a mingling of historic and bio-
graphic tints with the thread of the stories, to
connect them ineffaceably with the times and
places of their production, and with the person-
ality of the authors, so as to make them way-
marks, as it were, in any future and further study
of history or of geography.

Out of this effort and intention, has grown the
subject matter of this little book, which is planned
not alone for a pleasurable beguilement of time
in reviving memories of old stories, but for carrying effective knowledge of dates and places and
conditions which young people are blamable for
not knowing, and which if they come to know by
agreeable coupling of them with happy memories
of stories told at night, will stick all the faster and
firmer in memory.

I have not filled out my intention so well or so
richly as I could have hoped to do on beginning; but, such as it is, I hope the little book will

meet kindly greeting from many — scattered up
and down the country — who have kindred loves
for the work and the memory of the old story-
tellers.

CONTENTS.

ILLUSTRATIONS.

I.

INTRODUCTION.

Words to start with for Young Folks.

THE coach had come in at half-past four by the old clock that stood in the corner of the hall, and which had a dumpling-like face of a moon that slid itself into sight, by halves and quarters, in a most wonderful way. Half-past four of the afternoon it was, else we should not have been there to see, — nor to see the coach, which was another wonderful thing to behold; a round-bodied coach, hung upon enormous leathern thorough-braces, on which it went see-sawing over the bars upon the hill-sides of country roads. There was a door in the middle, with a miniature coach painted upon its panel, with horses in

full trot (making faster time than the coach ever did in
earnest), and over the painting was the legend, "Eclipse
Line." There was a rival "Express Line;" but the
"Eclipse" was our favorite. It had the best horses,
Harry said (he knew, Harry did); and the driver always
saved a place upon the coach-roof, back of his seat, and
this was what the "Express" driver never did, but
bundled us inside, with the women. Therefore we pat-
ronized the "Eclipse" line.

A great gulf of leather, behind the coach, received
the trunks, which were finished in that day with hairy
skins. Will Warner (of our school) had one which he
vowed was covered with a leopard-skin: it was certainly
spotted. Then, under the driver's seat of the "Eclipse"
was another cavernous recess for the carpet-bags and
small parcels; and again, upon the coach-roof, were hat-
boxes and band-boxes, kept from sliding off the fearful
height by a little iron railing of two bars, against which,
when the coach-top was free, — in vacation time, — we
planted our feet, and, with back to back, went swaying
and rollicking over the turnpike roads. There are no
such coach-loads now. I think there are no such
coaches. The Troy coach, known of hotel people and
of overland passengers, approaches it; but I am strongly
of opinion that the old New-England stage-coach had a
dignity and a character of its own, quite unapproachable
by any vehicle of these times. What ponderous cur-
tains, with their odor of varnish and paint! These all
were buttoned close upon that December afternoon;
and the sturdy wheels had such accumulation of half-
frozen mud over them, and around them, as to make
them strongly resemble the richly embossed chariot-

wheels that were figured in our book of Roman Anti-
quities.

And it *is* for us, on that day, a triumphal chariot.
We know what that queer-shaped box means upon the
coach-top, — not long enough, Harry hints, for bow and
arrows, which he had set his heart upon ; but there is
room in it for a Noah's ark, and balls, and battledoor,
and a "Boys' Own Book," and lots beside.   For uncle
Ned never makes
his Christmas visit
without a good stock
of such things.

And uncle Ned
is in the coach.
We see his earnest,
kindly face, and his
white locks floating
round it like a glory,
before   we   have
guessed at all the
riches   that   must
lie packed away in
the   Christmas-box
on the roof.   He
had a way of cud-
dling us youngsters

Uncle Ned.

in his lap we never forgot.   There was aunt Effie too,
with her queer old frontlet of curls, which she would
persist in wearing — though it would never compare
with her own sheen of silvery hair (we caught sight of
her sometimes in her chamber — so we knew about
that).   She was a goodly, fat woman, — was aunt Effie,

Harry said he loved fat women. Yet he has married since a woman as thin as a ghost: this is the way boyish opinions get overset in the hurly-burly of life.

But aunt Effie was as good as she was large. Every pat of her hand on our heads had the tender weight of all her heart in it. Not given to many words: perhaps because uncle Ned took all the talking to himself, for he fairly bubbled over with it.

We wondered if it was aunt Effie's way at home, by the privacy of her own fireside, to interject, as she did, into the swift current of uncle Ned's talk her approving or questioning "*Ed*waRDE!" I have tried to make the types show, with their capitals, how she uttered it; but even the capitals, rising in *crescendo* (you must look for that word in your Latin Dictionary), don't begin to figure the droll effect of her "*Ed*waRDE!"

Did these two dear old people ever love, — in the way of the story-books, — we wondered? Was there any billing and cooing? Had she ever a delicate little waist and golden ringlets, that "enraptured his regard"? At this date, I don't doubt it,— however much we all doubted it then.

They were childless people; perhaps that was the reason the big Christmas-box always came on time, and they with it. Aunt Effie, with all her love-pattings bestowed here and there, never failed to follow up the motions of uncle Ned, with a beaming eye; and he, good soul, never failed to look sharply after aunt Effie's comfort, or to take grace or caution from her "*Ed*waRDE!" as she happened to pronounce it.

Well — these good old childless souls had come to us, as I said, on this December day (the one before Christ-

mas), in the coach, which, with its rime of mud upon the
wheels, was so like a Roman triumphal chariot; and
the Christmas-box (big enough for any thing, except the
coveted bow and arrows) had been bestowed away for
the morrow's opening, and a royal supper had been
served, with a steaming dish of oysters from the creek
near by, and a fire had been kindled as early as three in
the afternoon in the great south sitting-room (Frank
and I bringing in the back-logs); and by seven or eight
o'clock we were all seated around it, waiting for uncle
Ned to begin.

He always told us a story on these visits. He always
had the same chair in the corner; and when he demurred
or halted at the start, or said he was old and rusty,
aunt Effie, from *her* corner, broke out upon him with
"*Ed*wARDE!"

With that, he began; since the first story-telling of his
I could remember — always with " Once upon a time."
I told Kitty, — who was a roly-poly dumpling of a cousin,
but *very* nice, — that it would be so now; and so it
was.

There is a delicious vagueness about "once upon a
time," that I think takes hold upon young listeners, —
if it does not upon the elderly ones. If we have an old
date in full, straightway the thing becomes historic, and
is brought to fast anchorage outside of the shadowy
realm into which it is so delightful — on Christmas Eve
— to wander. Again, if the story have its start-point
a few years ago, or a few months ago, it brings up the
thought of newspapers and news-mongers, from all
whose note-takings we cast loose delightsomely as we
drift out over that misty and indeterminate current of

gone-by years, which is shadowed forth darkly in —
"once upon a time."

Once upon a time, then ————————————

Once upon a Time.

But, bless you, I am not going to tell Uncle Ned's story here and now. I didn't promise it; and I have only led you along towards this pitch of expectation to show how much the conditions under which a story is told serve to fix it in mind. We always thought of Christmas and big fires, and the coach coming up, — sometimes it was a sleigh, to be sure, — and the gifts and the little listeners, when we thought of Uncle Ned's stories. And I think his stories — however humdrum they were (and I must confess, looking back upon them now, that some of them were terribly humdrum), were always the sweeter and the better for the surroundings under which they were told; and that we relish the memory of them now far more, because we knew the surroundings, and knew him, and all about him, and how kindly his meaning was, and how aunt Effie pushed him up to the work of it.

Well, I am to tell you now about other story-tellers not known in our family only, but known all over the world, far as English books ever go; and I want you to understand and remember some of the circumstances under which they told their stories; and who helped them on by calling out to them, and how they looked, and in what times they lived, and why they told such stories as they did.

And I want to tell you this not only because a knowledge of it will interest you more in the work of the old story-tellers, but because they were famous men and women, about whom you ought to know.

It is not much matter to learn if our uncle Ned came up on a coach, because his stories never reached very far, and he was not a man about whom the great world cares to know very much, — though they puzzle themselves to learn trifling things about men not half so honest, and true, and kind as he. But when it comes to Oliver Goldsmith, who told a story in such a way that all the world read it, and French and German and Italian people turned it into their own language, — why, it is well for you to know if there was an aunt Effie in his case, and stage-coaches; and if he lived in New England, or in Ireland; and what children he had, if any; and what became of him; and where he lies buried.

So of Jonathan Swift, another man I shall have to tell you about, who was a stronger man, but not half so kind-hearted; and was remembered by a great many people with a shudder; and yet who told a story so witty and so winning, about certain queer little folks, — not much larger than your thumb, — that you ought to know about him, and remember what his life was, when you read what he wrote.

Then, there are certain stories which in their way are very charming, about which we can't say positively just when they were written. But we can learn when they were first made generally known, and how they were handed down from year to year, and from generation to generation.

Of such are the fairy-stories belonging to all countries, and to the books of all nations, — stories to which children listen always with such open-eyed wonder.

Do the old people tell you there is harm in them? Well, it is a harm that must be met and conquered. We cannot root them out. The House that Jack built, it is hard to pull down. The gossips will be gossips. The evening shadows will throw grotesque lines on the greensward, that children will change into queer shapes.

And while we tell of them, and of the colors which story-tellers have put upon these strange shapes of unreal things, we will try and pluck all the harm out of them, by treating them as we would treat any other unreal shadows of things which are actual.

Those fairy-stories which have held their ground longest and best have almost always some good common-sense point in them ; and in no one that I can call to mind, do indolence and conceit win greater rewards than industry; or cunning and folly gain the battle over straightforward honesty.

Apollyon is a great, shining fellow in Bunyan's " Pilgrim's Progress ; " but the point of Christian's sword finds out the weak places in his harness of iron ; and under Great-Heart (which is a capital name for a hero), he goes down altogether, and is heard of no more.

Little Red Riding Hood may be eaten up by the wolf who has put on her grandmother's cap ; but the little Red Riding Hoods who are left will look all the sharper on those who are full of professions, and not judge people by their caps, and not believe the lying words of the strangers they meet upon the high-roads.

Such patient, quiet, steadfast toil as that of Cinderella, is apt to bring to those who are not fagged by it, and do not give it up, the most splendid of luck — slipper or no slipper. There may indeed be no marriage to a prince ; but there will be a marriage to Duty, which will be even grander and happier ; for Duty is always young, and never gets slip-shod, and never has bad humors.

Now, all these stories about which I have undertaken to tell you are printed stories ; and if there had been no way of printing them, you would never have heard of them or of the lesson of them ; and it is for this reason that I open my budget about the story-tellers, by saying something concerning the man who invented printing, and who, if he did not print the first book, certainly printed the first Bible.

You must not count upon great adventures and very extraordinary things as happening in all the chapters of this book : I dare say you will think some matters I have to talk about, very dull matters ; but I believe all the things I shall tell you will be worth your knowing, and will help your relish for the reading of the larger books which I shall speak of. You know we can't count upon a sunny day for every one of our summer picnics, nor always reckon upon a company of eager listeners for the stories we have to tell : it is very much to count on *one*.

One.

II.

FIRST PRINTERS AND THEIR HOMES.

The Dutchmen.

IN the year 1420 there was living in the city of Haarlem an old gentleman, who kept the keys of the cathedral, and who used, after dinner, to walk in the famous wood, that up to this time is growing just without the city walls. One day, while walking there, he found a very smooth bit of beech-bark, on which — as he was a handy man with his knife — he cut several letters so plainly and neatly, that after his return home he stamped them upon paper, and gave the paper to his boy as a "copy." After this, seeing that the thing had been neatly done, the old gentleman, whose name was Lawrence Coster, fell to thinking of what might be done with such letters cut in wood. By blackening them with ink, he made black stamps upon paper; and by dint of much thinking and much working, he came, in time, to the stamping of whole broadsides of letters, — which was really printing.

But before he succeeded in doing this well, he had found it necessary to try many experiments, and to take

27

into his employ several apprentices. He did his work very secretly, and told all of his apprentices to say nothing of the trials he was making. But a dishonest one among them, after a time, ran off from Holland into Germany, carrying with him a great many of the old gentleman's wooden blocks, and entire pages of a book which he was about to print.

This is the story that is told by an old Dutch writer, who was president of Haarlem College, and who printed his account a hundred and fifty years after Lawrence was robbed. He says he had the story from the lips of most respectable old citizens, who had heard it from their fathers ; and, furthermore, he says that he had a teacher in his young days, who had known, long before, an old servant of Lawrence Coster's ; and this servant would burst into tears whenever he spoke of the way in which his poor master was robbed, and so lost the credit of his discovery.

The Dutch writers believe this story, and hint that the runaway apprentice was John Faust, or John Gutenberg ; but the Germans justly say there is no proof of this. It is certain, however, that there was a Lawrence (*Custos*, or Keeper, of the cathedral), who busied himself with stamping letters, and with engraving. His statue is on the market-place in Haarlem, and his rough-looking books are, — some of them, — now in the "State House" of Haarlem. They are dingy, and printed with bad ink, and seem to have been struck from large engraved blocks, and not from movable types. They are without any date ; but people learned in such matters think they belong to a period somewhat earlier than any book of Faust, or of Gutenberg, who are commonly called the discoverers of printing.

John Gutenberg.

John Gutenberg, at the very time when this old Dutchman was experimenting with his blocks in Holland, was also working in *his* way, very secretly, in a house that was standing not many years ago in the ancient city of Strasburg. He had two working partners, who were bound by oath not to reveal the secret of the arts he was engaged upon. But one of these partners died; and upon this, his heirs claimed a right to know the secrets of Gutenberg. Gutenberg refused; and there was a trial of the case, some account of which was discovered more than three hundred years afterward in an old tower of Strasburg.

This trial took place in the year 1439. Gutenburg was not forced to betray his secret; but it did appear, from the testimony of the witnesses, that he was occupied with some way of making books (or manuscripts) cheaper than they had ever been made before.

But Gutenberg was getting on so poorly at Strasburg, and lost so much money in his experiments, that he went away to Mayence, which is a German city farther down the Rhine. He there formed a partnership with a rich silversmith named John Faust, who took an oath of secrecy, and supplied him with money, on condition that after a certain time it should be repaid to him.

Then Gutenberg set to work in earnest. Some accounts say he had a brother who assisted him; and the Dutch writers think this brother may have been the robber of poor Lawrence Coster. But there is no proof of it; and it is too late to find any proof now. There

was certainly a Peter Schöffer, a scribe, or designer, who
worked for Gutenberg, and who finished up his first
books by drawing lines around the pages, and making
ornamental initial letters, and filling up gaps in the

Trying the Type.

printing.   This Schöffer was a shrewd fellow, and
watched Gutenberg very closely.   He used to talk over
what he saw, and what he thought, with Faust.   He
told Faust he could contrive better types than Gutenberg was using; and, acting on his hints, Faust, who

was a skilful worker in metals, run types in a mould; and these were probably the first *cast* types ever made. These promised so well that Faust determined to get rid of Gutenberg, and to carry on the business with Schöffer — to whom he gave his only daughter Christine for a wife.

Faust called on Gutenberg for his loan shortly after, which Gutenberg couldn't pay; and in consequence he had to give up to Faust all his tools, his presses, and his unfinished work, among which was a Bible nearly two-thirds completed. This, Faust and Schöffer hurried through, and sold as a manuscript. They sold it as a manuscript, because manuscripts brought high prices, and because if it were known that this Bible was made in some easier and cheaper way, they could not be sure of so good a price; and besides, this would make people curious to find out about this easier way of making books, which Faust and Schöffer wished to keep secret.

There are two copies in the National Library at Paris; one copy at the Royal Library at Munich; and one at Vienna. It is not what is commonly known as the Mayence Bible, but is of earlier date than that.

It is without name of printer or publisher, and without date. It is in two great volumes folio, of about six hundred pages a volume. You very likely could not read a word of it if you were to see it; for it is in Latin, and in black Gothic type, with many of the words abbreviated, and packed so closely together as to puzzle the eye. I give a line of this printing to show you that it would not make easy reading. Should you chance to own a copy (and you probably never will), you could sell it for enough money to buy yourself a little library of about two thousand volumes.

genuit ezechiam:ezechias aũt genuit

It was certainly the first Bible printed from movable
types ; but poor Gutenberg got no money from it,
though he had done most of the work upon it.   But he
did not grow disheartened.   He toiled on, though he
was without the help of Schöffer and of Faust, and in a
few years afterward succeeded in making books which
were as good as those of his rivals.   Before he died his
name was attached to books printed as clearly and
sharply as books are printed to-day.

Of course they are very proud of his memory in the
old Rhine town of Mayence, where he labored ; and
they have erected a statue there to his memory, — from
a design by the great Danish sculptor, Thorwaldsen.
This statue was erected in August, 1837 ; and there
was a great festival on the occasion — fifteen thousand
people crowding into the town to assist in doing honor
to the memory of the first printer.   The old cathedral
was thronged ; the Bishop of Mayence said high mass ;
and the first Bible printed by Gutenberg was displayed.
On the site where he worked there is now a club-house ;
and the gentlemen of the club-house have erected
another little statue to Gutenberg in the inner court
of their building.

The City of Strasburg.

But Strasburg is as proud of him as Mayence ; for in
Strasburg the burghers of that city say he studied out
the plans which he afterward carried into execution

The Guttenberg Monument at Strasburg.

at Mayence. So in Strasburg, in 1840, they erected another statue to his memory, by David, a French sculptor. It is of bronze, and is one of the imposing sights of the city — as you may see from the picture I have given of it.

I have a little copy of the head of Gutenberg as he is represented in this statue, in plaster and wax, which I brought away from Strasburg a great many years ago. It is before me as I write, — a cap trimmed with fur upon the head, a sober and most comely face, a long beard which would have become a Hebrew patriarch. He must have been a man of noble presence ; and, though we know but very little of his personal history, it is certain that his name and his fame will live among those of the greatest inventors. Every book you read is a monument to his memory ; and he is deserving of most kindly remembrance, because he busied himself throughout a long life, in making serviceable an art which is of the greatest benefit to everybody. Those who made dictionaries of biography in the centuries which followed closely after him didn't think it worth their while to gather up any facts about his life, or even to mention him ; but they spent a great deal of useless labor in inquiries about the lives of petty princes who made wars for conquest, and of students who made wars with words, for conquest in some petty points of theology ; but these princes and bookworms are forgotten now, while John Gutenberg in that noble statue of the old city of Strasburg is looked upon, and thought of, and honored, more than if Dr. Bayle had written one of his longest and fullest folio pages about him.

You will see the statue if you ever go to Strasburg ;

and you will see the cathedral too, which is one of the grandest and most beautiful of Europe. The tallest spire in New York would hardly reach half way to its top; and four or five country church towers, if piled one upon the other, would not make a scaffolding high enough to reach the middle of its spire. I give a glimpse of it, as you see it over the quaint roofs of the city, in order that you may associate it with the story of the first printer.

Strasburg Cathedral.

You will see that only one of its towers bears a spire: upon the top of the shorter tower there is a little cottage of entertainment, more than two hundred feet above the level of the pavement. Here, those who venture on a climb to this lofty plateau may rest, and consider — if they will mount still higher into the regions of air, where the great spire will carry them if they choose to go.

Some thirty years ago I tried this second climbing; but the stone-work is as open as a lattice, and the people on the street far below looked like pygmies, and the whole city and spire seemed to reel with me; and such a degree of dizziness crept over me, that I was glad to get down again to what seemed the solid footing of the deck of the tower.

And was the great cathedral there when Gutenberg was worrying over his types in that ancient city? Yes: Gutenberg saw it; very likely he saw some of the last stones placed upon the tower; for though it was commenced three or four centuries before, and was in course of building when Wallace was fighting so bravely in the glens of Scotland (about which you will remember, if you have read "The Scottish Chiefs"), the tower was only completed in 1365.

Another thing to remember about this great cathedral, which throws its shadow upon Gutenberg's statue, is, — Sabina Erwin of Steinbach, a daughter of the great architect, conducted and directed the building of much of it in the years when it was being finished. Think of that when you hear that women can do no grand things! Think, too, that in those very years, when Gutenberg was printing his first book, that other wonderful woman Joan of Arc, was putting courage into French armies by leading them herself, — and the first printer was very likely one of those who grieved greatly when they learned that the poor, brave Joan had been burned in the city of Rouen, by order of the cruel English commander.

I don't think that Gutenberg ever saw the clock that you may now see in the Cathedral of Strasburg, for it has only been there a little over three hundred years. But it is a famous clock: I would not dare to tell you of all the amazing things its hidden machinery can do. The figures of the apostles march; a cock claps his wings, and crows; death (in the shape of a skeleton) appears; and there are chimes, and sweet jangling sounds; and the moon shows its changes, and the planets too.

But, most of all, think, — in connection with this great church building and the clock and the spire, and the rich *patés de foie gras* which they give you for dinner in Strasburg, — think of the old long-bearded prince of printers, who by his art and toil and genius contrived movable types, and first made it possible for all the men who can tell stories worth a long life, to repeat them in print, so that you may take them in your hand to study, and dream over, and enjoy.

Old English Printers.

But who printed the first English book? And did that follow quickly afterward? Not many years — perhaps twenty. And the man who did this was named William Caxton — a name which has been held in very great honor ever since.

He was in early life apprentice to a seller of dry-goods in London ; but he was an excellent apprentice ; and his master came to be Mayor of London, and left him a fair fortune. His zeal and industry made him a marked man, — so that he was sent by the Government over to Flanders, to the city of Bruges, where Philip the Good of Burgundy was ruling. And there he studied, and there he came to a knowledge of what Gutenberg had been doing, and of what Faust had been doing, in Mayence. And he translated the "Histories of Troye" — for he had made himself a good scholar ; and he secured some of the workmen who had been with Faust and Schöffer, after their printing-office was broken up by a war that raged in that day along the Rhine ; and, taking over the workmen into England, he set up a printing-office at Westminster, — in some outbuilding of the famous Westminster Abbey, — and there printed his Histories of Troye, and many another book ; among them a Life of Charles the Great, of which he says, "I have specially reduced it (translated it) after the simple cunning that God hath lent to me, whereof I humbly and with all my heart thank Him, and also am bounden to pray for my fathers and mothers souls, that in my youth set me to school, by which, by the sufferance of God, I get my living I hope truly."

And in this spirit of old-fashioned honesty and zeal, the good printer toiled all the days of his life.

And after his death, the men who had worked with him — of whom Wynkyn de Worde was chief — carried on labor in the same spirit, and looked forward to "the happy day when a Bible should be chained in every church, for every Christian man to look upon."

And this was a great thing to look forward to in that day. Books had borne and were bearing a value which would astonish you now. An old Italian called Poggio had — in those centuries, and not long before — exchanged his manuscript copy of Livy for a country villa near to Florence.

In England, the cost of copying a book in writing was worth the price of two fat oxen. Chaining books to desks was not uncommon; but it was not in every church they were chained. They were in great religious houses, called monasteries and abbeys; or they were carefully guarded in the cabinets of kings.

The bindings of many of the old manuscript books, and of the early printed ones, were enriched with very rare carving in ivory or wood, or they were enamelled beautifully on copper and adorned with pearls and rare stones, and their clasps were of silver and of gold. Many bindings of this sort are now kept with great care in European museums, and are very much valued. In the old church of Monza, which is an Italian town very near to Milan, there is a very old and curious piece of book-binding, which, with its manuscript of the Gospels in Greek, was given to the church by Theodolinda, a good and famous queen of the Lombards, who lived twelve hundred years ago. It is of silver and gold, and set over with precious stones, and is, I think, the oldest bound book in the world. It was a very old book, and a prized book, when Wynkyn de Worde talked about chaining a Bible, some day, in every church.

What would the good old man have thought of Bibles printed and sold for only a few pennies each? What would the first English printer have thought, if he had been told that within three centuries, in a country unheard of by him (for Columbus sailed on his first voyage the very year on which William Caxton died), and in a single city of that country, more type would be set up in one day, than was set up in all Europe during the space of a year, in his time?

III.

THE ARABIAN NIGHTS

Who wrote the Stories?

WHO knows? Not Captain Mayne Reid; though had he been born a Persian, and lived long time enough ago, and been a Caliph with a long beard and a cimiter — instead of a captain in the Mexican war, with a Colt's revolver and a goatee, — and had he seen the cloud of dust which Ali-Baba saw, I think he could have made out the band of forty robbers under it, and the cave, and all the rest.

But Mayne Reid didn't see the cloud of dust which covered those robbers (and which is very apt to cover all gangs of public robbers), and did not live so long ago, and therefore did not write "The Arabian Nights." Nor did Mrs. Hannah More, for the book is not in her style; nor did the author of "Little Women."

You could never guess who wrote "The Arabian Nights," — for nobody knows when those stories were first written. It seems very odd that a book should be made, and no one able to tell when it was made. The publishers don't allow such things to happen nowadays. Yet it is even so with the book we are talking of. Of course it is possible to fix the date of the many translations of "The Arabian Nights" which have been made into the languages of Europe from the old Arabic manuscripts. Thus it was in the year 1704 that a certain Antoine Galland, a distinguished Oriental scholar of Paris, who had travelled in the East, and who had collected many curious manuscripts and medals, published a French translation of what was called "The Thousand and One Nights." This was in the time of the gay court of Louis the Fourteenth ; and the fine ladies of the court — those of them who could read — all devoured the book ; and the school-boys throughout France (though there were not many school-boys in those days outside of the great cities) all came to know the wonderful stories of Aladdin and of Ali-Baba. Remember that this was about the time when the great Duke of Marlboro' was winning his famous victories on the Continent, — specially that of Blenheim ; about which an English poet, Dr. Southey, has written a quaint little poem, which you should read. It was in the lifetime, too, of Daniel Defoe, — who wrote that ever-charming story of Robinson Crusoe some twelve or fourteen years later ; and the first newspaper in America — called "The Boston News Letter" — was printed in the same year in which Antoine Galland published his translation of "The Thousand and One Nights." If you should go to Paris, and be curious to see it, you can find in the Imperial Library, or the National Library (or whatever those changeable French people may call it now), the very manuscript of Antoine Galland.

Some years afterward there was a new and fuller translation by another Oriental scholar, who had succeeded M. Galland as professor of Arabic in the Royal College. Then there followed, in the early part of this century, translations into English; and I suppose that American boys in the days of President Monroe took their first taste of those gorgeous Arabian tales.

But the completest of all the collections was made by a German scholar, Mr. Von Hammer, in the year 1824 — not so far back but that your fathers and mothers may remember little stray paragraphs in the papers, which made mention of how a German scholar had traced these old Arabian tales back to a very dim antiquity in India; and how he believed they had thence gone into Persia, where the great men of the stories all became Caliphs; and how they floated thence, by hearsay, into Arabia (which was a country of scribes and scholars in the days of Haroun al Raschid); and how they there took form in the old Arabic manuscripts which Antoine Galland had found and translated. But during the century that had passed since M. Galland's death, other and fuller Arabic copies had been found, with new tales added, and with other versions of the tales first told.

But what we call the machinery of the stories was always much the same; and the same Genii flashed out in smoke and flame, and the same cimiters went blazing and dealing death through all the copies of "The Thousand and One Nights."

But why came that title of "The Thousand and One Nights," which belonged, and still belongs, to all the European collections of these old Arabian stories? I

will tell you why; and in telling you why, I shall give
you the whole background on which all these various
Arabian stories, wherever found, are arrayed. And the
background is itself a story, and this is the way it
runs : —

The Vizier's Daughter.

Once there lived a wicked Sultan of Persia, whose
name was Schahriar; and he had many wives — like
the Persian Shah who went journeying into England a
few summers ago; and he thought of his wives as stock-
owners think of their cattle — and I fear the present
Persian Shah thinks no otherwise.

Well, when this old Schahriar found that his wives
were faithless and deceitful, — as all wives will be who
are esteemed no more than cattle, — he vowed that he
would cut off all chance of their sinning by making
an end of them: so it happened that whatever new
wife he espoused one day, he killed upon the next.

You will think the brides were foolish to marry him ;
but many women keep on making as foolish matches all
the world over; and she who marries a sot, or the man
who promises to be a sot, is killed slowly, instead of
being killed quickly with a bow-string, — as the Schahriar did his work.

Besides, all women of the East were slaves, as they
are mostly now, and subject to whatever orders the
Sultan might make.

Now, it happened that this old Schahriar had a vizier,
or chief officer under him, who executed all his murderous orders, and who was horrified by the cruelties
he had to commit. And this same vizier had a beauti-

ful and accomplished daughter, who was even more
horrified than her father; and she plotted how she
might stay the bloody actions of the Schahriar.

Vizier and Daughter.

She could gain no access to him, and could hope to
win no influence over him, except by becoming his
bride; but, if she became his bride, she would have but
one day to live. So, at least, thought her sisters and

her father. She, of course, found it very hard to win
the consent of her father, the vizier, to her plan; but at
last she succeeded, and so arranged matters that the
Schahriar should command her to be his bride.

The fatal marriage-day came, and the vizier was in an
agony of grief and alarm. The morning after the
espousals, he waited — in an ecstasy of fear — the
usual order for the slaughter of the innocent bride ; but
to his amazement and present relief, the order was
postponed to the following day.

This bride, whose name was Scheherazade, — known
now to school-boys and school-girls all over the world,
— was most beguiling of speech, and a most charming
story-teller. And on the day of her marriage she had
commenced the narration of a most engrossing story to
her husband the Schahriar; and had so artfully timed it,
and measured out its length, that, when the hour came
for the Sultan to set about his cares of office, she should
be at its most interesting stage. The Sultan had been
so beguiled by the witchery of her narrative, and so
eager to learn the issue, that he put off the execution
of his murderous design, in order to hear the termina-
tion of the story on the following night.

And so rich was the narration, and so great was the
art of the princess Scheherazade, that she kept alive
the curiosity and wonder of her husband, the Sultan,
— day after day, and week after week, and month after
month, — until her fascinating stories had lasted for a
thousand and one nights.

If you count up these you will find they make a
period of two years and nine months — during which
she had beguiled the Sultan, and stayed the order for

her execution. In the interval, children had been born
to her; and she had so won upon her husband, that he
abolished his cruel edict forever, — on condition that
from time to time she should tell over again those
enchanting stories. And the stories she told on those
thousand and one nights, and which have been recited
since in every language of Europe, thousands and thousands of times, are the Arabian Nights tales.

If this account is not true in all particulars, it is at
least as true as the stories are.

A good woman sacrificed herself to work a deed of
benevolence. *That* story, at any rate, is true, and is
being repeated over and over in lives all around us.

But, after all, the question is not answered as to who
wrote "The Arabian Nights." I doubt if it ever will be
answered truly. Who cares, indeed? I dare say that
youngsters in these days of investigation committees
are growing up more curious and inquiring than they
used to be; but I know well I cared or thought nothing about the authorship in those old school days when
I caught my first reading of Aladdin and the Wonderful
Lamp.

What a night it was! What a feast! I think I could
have kissed the hand that wrote it.

A little red morocco-bound book it was, with gilt
edges to the leaves, that I had borrowed from Tom
Spooner; and Tom Spooner's aunt had loaned it to him,
and she thought all the world of it, and had covered it
in brown paper, and I mustn't soil it, or dog's-ear it.
And I sat down with it — how well I remember! — at a
little square-legged red table in the north recitation-
room at E—— school; and there was a black hole in

the top of the table — where Dick Linsey, who was a
military character, and freckled, had set off a squib of
gunpowder (and got trounced for it) ; and the smell of
the burnt powder lingered there, and came up grateful-
ly into my nostrils, as I read about the sulphurous
clouds rolling up round the wonderful lamp, and the
Genie coming forth in smoke and flames !

What delight ! If I could only fall in with an old
peddler with a rusty lamp, — such as Aladdin's, —
wouldn't I rub it !

And with my elbows fast on the little red table, and
my knees fast against the square legs, and the smell of
the old squib regaling me, I thought what I would
order the Genie to do, if I ever had a chance : — A
week's holiday to begin with ; and the Genie should be
requested to set the school "principal" down, green
spectacles and all, in the thickest of the woods somewhere on the "mountain." Saturday afternoons should
come twice a week — at the very least ; turkey, with
stuffing, every day except oyster day. I would have a
case of pocket-knives "Rogers' superfine cutlery" —
(though Kingsbury always insisted that "Wosten-
holm's" were better) brought into my closet, and would
give them out, cautiously, to the clever boys. I would
have a sled, brought by the Genie, that would beat
Ben Brace's "Reindeer," he bragged so much about, —
by two rods, at least. I would have a cork jacket, with
which I could swim across Snipsic Lake, where it was
widest, — twice over, — and think nothing of it. I
would have a cavern, like the salt mines in Cracow,
Poland (as pictured in Parley's Geography) ; only, instead of salt, it should all be rock-candy ; and I would

let in clever fellows and pretty girls, and the homely
ones, too — well, as often as every Wednesday.

Ah, well-a-day! we never come to the ownership of
such caverns! We never find a peddler with the sort
of lamp that will bring any sort of riches — with wishing.

But, my youngsters, there is a Genie that will come
to any boy's command, and will work out amazing
things for you all through boyhood, and all through
life ; and his name is — Industry.

And now, if your lessons are all done, and if you
will keep in mind what I have said about " The Arabian
Nights," and their history, we will have a taste of these
Eastern stories.

Aladdin and his Lamp.

Aladdin was the son of a poor old woman who lived
in a city of China. His father was dead, and he didn't
work as he should have done to support his old mother :
in fact, all his early life was not the sort of one out of
which men are apt to grow into heroes.

He was idling in the streets one day — as idle fellows
will — when he met a strange man with a dark face,
who asked Aladdin his name, and told him he was a
relative of his father's, and would befriend him ; and
thereupon he gave him some gold coins, with which
Aladdin ran off home.

After a few days this strange man (who was a magician
— though Aladdin couldn't know that) met the boy again,
and gave him more money, and paid a visit to his old
mother, and promised to set up the boy in trade, which

he did do — furnishing him silks to sell, or whatever
the city people would be apt to buy. And this same
strange dark man used to take Aladdin about the city,
and show him all the wonderful sights ; and finally led
him one day far beyond the city walls, to a retired place
between two mountains. There with the help of Aladdin he builds a fire (a great many of the wonders of
these tales turn upon the secret power of fire) ; then he
utters a few magical words, and the ground opens, showing an iron plate, which Aladdin lifts, and lo ! there
appear steps going down into a cavern in the earth.

The magician instructs Aladdin how he is to descend,
— tells him what halls of treasure he will pass through,
and gardens with splendid fruit, — tells him how he
must touch nothing till he reaches the farthest chamber,
where he will find an iron lamp in a niche of the wall.
This he must seize upon, and bring back : after he has
secured this, he may pluck as much of the fruit as he
chooses. Lastly he puts on the boy's finger a ring,
which will give him safety and help.

So Aladdin enters, — marches through the great glit-
tering corridors (which, though they were deep under
ground, were as light as day), — passes through the gardens, and reaches and seizes the lamp.

He picks some of the fruit in the garden ; but what
seemed fruit are only topazes and diamonds and pearls.
Of course he fills his purse and his pockets ; and, arrived at the steps, the magician asks him to hand up
the lamp.

But Aladdin is cautious : perhaps he suspects a little
false play on the part of the magician, and he refuses
until he shall have come fairly out.

At this the magician in a rage utters again a few magical words, and the ground and iron door close on poor Aladdin. He wanders in despair up and down. He calls out; but who can hear him in those depths? At last he betakes himself to prayer; and, in the act of clasping his hands, he rubs slightly the ring upon his finger. Upon this a great Genie appears in smoke and flame, by whose power he is placed outside once more, and he wanders back to his mother's house in the city.

I don't know what became of his shop and stock of goods; or what became of his pocket-full of rubies and diamonds. The story doesn't say; but it does say that he felt hungry on one occasion, when there was no bread in the house, and no money. So he determined to sell the old lamp: the mother thinks no one will buy it, except she brighten it up a little. But she has no sooner set to work at the scouring, than smoke and flame fill the place, and out of the smoke and flame comes a terrible Genie, who offers to do Aladdin's bidding.

Aladdin wants food; and straightway, the Genie having vanished, slaves come in from some unknown quarter, and bring silver and gold dishes heaped up with meats and fruits such as these humble people had never tasted before. And when after some days the meats are gone, the gold dishes are sold to a Jew, and they have money for months longer. Two or three times in the course of a year this is repeated: the lamp is rubbed; the Genie comes; the food in golden dishes is sent up; the dishes are sold. I don't think Aladdin can have made a very good bargain with the Jew who bought his dishes. For my part, I think I should have

commanded the Genie to bring a good batch of "cur
rent funds," and bought my own dishes. But Aladdin
didn't.

He began shortly to have ambitious views about getting up in the world. He had seen the Sultan's daughter, and, approving of her looks, thought he would like
to marry her. He sent his old mother to "interview"
the Sultan on the subject.

People at the court hooted her at the first; but she
bore great gifts of jewels and gold, — so great that at
last the Sultan listened, and promised that at the end of
a certain time his daughter would receive the addresses
of this unknown lover.

But, as the Sultan had already the rare jewels in his
own keeping, he did not keep very fast in mind poor
Aladdin; and so Aladdin woke one morning to hear the
bells ringing for the marriage of the Sultan's daughter.
However, by the aid of the lamp and the Genie, he put
difficulties in the way of this new marriage; and sent
such splendid gifts that at last he won his purpose; and
his marriage day with the beautiful daughter of the
Sultan was really appointed. He built a magnificent
palace — all through the Genie of the lamp — in which
he was to live; and he purposely left one window in the
great hall unfinished, and then he challenged the best
work-people of the Sultan to complete it.

The Sultan sent his cunningest workmen, and his
whole stock of jewels, to make the window of the
palace as perfect as the rest. But they could not do it.
The laborers were not cunning enough, and the jewels
were not rare enough. So Aladdin ordered them away;
and then (with his lamp, and a little rubbing of it) he
called his Genie, and all was finished in an hour's time.

The Sultan's daughter seems to have liked Aladdin; and they lived very happily together for a while in this palace. I dare say the old people of the court thought Aladdin an upstart, and perhaps they didn't visit him notwithstanding his wife's position.

Meantime, what has become of that African magician? He had gone away — across Tartary possibly, and by way of Bagdad very likely, to his own country, — thinking poor Aladdin was buried in the cavern. But, by his magic, he learned after a time how things had turned in China: so he travelled back to get possession of the wonderful lamp. The way in which he did this was a very shrewd way; for he disguised himself as a peddler of new and flash trinkets, and offered to change them for old candlesticks or old lamps.

If he had lived in our time, he would have found that women love old candlesticks very much more than any new things; but it was not so then; and he went to the gates of this splendid Aladdin palace, bawling his wares, and offering to change new lamps for old ones. And some slave — I suppose an upper chambermaid — reported what he said to the princess Buddir al Buddoor (which was the name of Aladdin's bride). And she hinted to the princess that an old lamp stood always on her master's table, which was so ugly and old, that it would be much better to have a new one in place of it.

The princess Buddir thought the same; and, Aladdin being away a-hunting, the bargain was made.

What do you think came of it? Why, next morning, when the Sultan waked up, he looked over to admire the fine palace of his son-in-law, and behold! there was no palace there! The African magician (by the aid of the lamp) had whisked it away into his own country.

Poor Aladdin, when he came back from hunting, had a sorry time of it, and the Sultan threatened to take off his head. But he begged grace for two months or so, in which time he hoped to get things straight again. What way should he turn? He knew it must all come of the lamp; but where to find it? He thought if he could discover the princess, he might learn something about the lamp; though I am afraid he lamented the loss of the lamp more than he did the loss of the princess. He remembered the ring the magician had given him, and gave it a good rubbing; sure enough, the old Genie that had met him in the cavern came back in smoke and flame. The Genie couldn't give back his bride to him; but it transported him over land and sea in a twinkling, and set him down under the walls of his lost palace, which was standing now in the magician's country, just as complete and beautiful as it stood before in China. This was very wonderful. I suppose if the African newspapers of that time remarked upon it, they probably said, — "We observe that a fine residence has gone up on Pyramid Street, adding much to the value of property in that locality, and doing credit to the taste and enterprise of our fellow townsman Mr. Magic."

Aladdin saw through the blinds of a window of the residence the beloved Buddir (I suppose he called her Budd, or perhaps Rosebud); and she saw him, and sent her maid to open the postern, or whatever the gate was called; and he came in, and learned how it had all happened. And Rosebud said the magician came every day, and was trying to win her affections. Aladdin told her not to bluff him outright; but to treat him

kindly, and ask him to take supper with her. Then he
goes to a drug-shop near by, and buys a powder, —
sulphate of morphia, perhaps, — and, returning quietly
and secretly, causes the powder to be put in the magician's cup.

That is the end of the magician. The lamp — as you
will have guessed — was in his bosom ; and Aladdin
takes it out — rubs it, and whisks his palace — Rosebud and all — back to China once more.

The Sultan is delighted to find things on their old
footing. And I suppose the China newspapers said,
" We are gratified to see that the residence of our friend
Col. Aladdin is again in position, and occupied by the
esteemed family of the colonel. Its temporary dis-
placement is said to have been due to a slight earth-
quake, against which in future we understand that the
colonel has abundantly provided. Mrs. Col. Aladdin,
née Buddir, is, we learn, in her usual health, not having
suffered, as was at first reported, by the catastrophe."

Things were now going on very swimmingly with
Aladdin ; and they would have continued thus, had not
an old lady who boasted of being very religious (which
is not a thing to boast of) put herself in the way of
Princess Budd, and so won upon her, that Rosebud
thought she would do nothing without taking the advice
of Fatima, — which was the name of the pretended
holy woman.

Rosebud asked Fatima how she liked her palace, and
her crockery, and her great Hall. Fatima liked it all
very well, except the Hall, which she thought wanted a
Roc's egg hung up in the middle.

It must have been a very great hall ; for a Roc's egg

was so large that when it lay upon the plain it looked
like a round-topped temple.

But perhaps Budd had never seen one — probably not.
She asked Aladdin to get her a Roc's egg. So he takes
to his lamp, and calls up his Genie.

For once the Great Slave was raging with anger.
The house shook; flames darted from the eyes of the
Genie. Aladdin did not know that the Roc was own
cousin to this creature of smoke and flame — and that
they were much attached to each other.

Roc's Egg.

The Genie at last cooled down, and told Aladdin how
it was; and told him, besides, that the holy woman was
no woman at all — only a brother of the wicked magician, who had murdered the true Fatima, and had made
his way into the palace to destroy Aladdin, and get possession of the Wonderful Lamp.

So Aladdin determined to meet the tricks of the
magician with a trick of his own. He pretended to be
sick, and summoned the holy woman to comfort him:
he watched her narrowly, and saw that under the folds

of her gown she had a dagger in hand. Seizing his chance, he snatched it from her, and plunged it in her bosom ; and that was the end of the other magician.

Rosebud was greatly shocked ; for she thought still it was Fatima who was murdered. She dried her tears when Aladdin told her the true story. And ever after they lived together in great comfort, and kept the Wonderful Lamp till they died.

And who do you think has the Lamp now ? Nobody knows.

It seems strange that such a lazy, good-for-nothing fellow as Aladdin is said to be in the beginning of the story, should have come to such great luck. Such boys in our day don't come to any thing good or great. The only way I can account for it is — by supposing that there was really no lamp at all, and that the old story-teller intended what he calls the Lamp to mean — only Industry and Watchfulness — which, as long as Aladdin kept and used, brought him riches and honor ; and whenever he lost hold on them — every thing turned out badly.

A Great Traveller.

In the time of the great Haroun al Raschid ———
You don't know who the great Haroun al Raschid was ?

He was a real Eastern monarch, surnamed The Just, who lived about eleven hundred years ago in Bagdad. He loved science, and loved letters ; he loved fair women, and he loved pearls and jewels.

I don't know if all is true that the histories tell about

him ; but he must have been a grand monarch, and lived in more luxury than most monarchs.

I can't forget the stories of him, which an old teacher of my boyish days put in my mind. They cling so to my memory, that I never hear the sweetly-flowing name of Haroun al Raschid, but I seem to see great gardens full of bloom, and thrones with jewels crusted on them, and sparkling fountains, and flashing swords, and silken turbans, and troops of camels, and palm-trees lifting their tops into the dreamy haze of Eastern countries. Then, again, I see the great Caliph seated on his jewelled throne, and the Grand Vizier, Jaeffer, in attendance on him — looking lovingly upon the beautiful face of the Princess — the daughter of Haroun. Poor Jaeffer! He came to look too lovingly upon the beautiful face of the Princess; and the great Caliph clipped off his head with a cimeter. This is history I am telling you now ; and this really and truly happened. It has made a great blot upon the fame of Haroun al Raschid, who, — for all this, was the most brilliant and the justest monarch of those centuries ; and he lived in the age of Charlemagne.

Well — it was in the time of this great Caliph Haroun al Raschid, and in his great city of Bagdad, that a porter named Hindbad, very poor, and very tired, and very hungry, — one day sat at the gate of a rich, tall palace, snuffing the odors of the rich dinner that was being served within.

The by-standers told him he was at the door of the great traveller and merchant — Sindbad. But it did not console the poor fellow to know that the rich man had a name almost like his own.

"Alas!" said he (nobody says "Alas!" now, whatever happens), "Alas, why has Allah, the great God, given to this man plenty, and to poor Hindbad only poverty?"

Some one of the by-standers — very likely the door-keeper — reported this speech of the poor fellow to Sindbad; and Sindbad ordered him brought in, and gave him a place at his table, and then and there commenced the story of those dangerous voyages of his, and of those trials and labors, which had made him rich. I suppose he wanted to make poor Hindbad

Street of Bagdad.

understand that riches do not fall from the clouds, and that very many who enjoy them have come to them through long struggles and dangers — if nothing worse.

Sindbad said that he was the son of a merchant; and that on his first voyage he was one day becalmed beside what seemed a great green island; and that he, with several of the crew, went ashore, and after wandering about some time suddenly felt the land quake and heave under them. This was not strange; for what they had taken to be an island was in reality only the back of a huge sea-monster sleeping on the water. Before he had fairly rolled over and gone down, most of the men made their escape in the boat; but poor Sindbad was not quick enough, so he was overwhelmed in the sea. Luckily he seized upon a log as he rose, and clambering upon it, floated upon it a day and a night, and at last was swept into the bay of a real island where he had many adventures, but ended with getting home safely, and with the wonderful recovery of all the goods he had taken out in his ship.

On his second voyage he was cast away again; and upon the island where he landed he came upon one of those wonderful Roc's eggs of which a picture was given you a little way back. Of course he had no idea what it could be; but while he gazed upon it in wonderment the sky was darkened, and the mother-bird came sailing to her nest. He was so near the egg, that the great Roc (which was large enough to carry off an elephant in its claws) sat down upon her egg and poor Sindbad. He made himself as small as he could; and then with some cord he had in his pocket — what does he do but lash himself to the ankle, or to one of the toes, of the great bird!

Was there ever such a bird? To tell truth, I don't think Sindbad's story is very good authority; but there was an old Venetian traveller named Marco Polo, who went all across Asia some years later than the time of Haroun, and he says he heard of the Roc; and people told him it could carry up an elephant and a rhinoceros together. But then, Marco Polo, though he was a real traveller, told some stories that it is hard to believe.

Why did Sindbad tie himself to the leg of the great Roc? The truth is, there was nothing to eat on the great plain where the Roc's nest was; and he was so badly off, that he thought he could not fare worse in

going wherever the Roc might take him. He doesn't
seem to have been at all afraid that the Roc would
devour him; and he had as good a reason for wishing
to change his place of residence as many people have
now every May-day.

Roc.

The Roc, when it flew, took him up, — so high, he
could see no ground: he was swept through the clouds,
and great clouds were below him. Then at last,
swooping down in great circles over sea and over land,
the Roc alighted in a barren valley hemmed in on all
sides by high mountains. From the account Sindbad
gave of it, it must have been very much like the famous
valley of Yosemite in California. Yet I don't think it
was the Yosemite. However, he untied himself hastily;
and presently after, the Roc, having taken up a huge
serpent in his beak, soared away.

Sindbad found himself without food. There were
no houses in this mountain valley; there were no
fruits; huge serpents in plenty, and — strange to say
— great store of diamonds scattered all over the sur-

face of the ground. But all around him the cliffs were so steep that there was no hope of climbing away ; least of all, if he should load himself with diamonds. It was a dreadful night he passed after his air-voyage tied to the leg of the Roc. There was no shelter except in a crevice of the cliffs — too narrow for the great serpents to creep in. The next day, as he wandered about, faint with hunger, he suddenly felt a shock of something falling on the ground near him ; and, on looking carefully, he found that this falling matter was nothing less than big rounds of uncooked beef. He saw, too, that these fragments of meat were directly pounced upon by gigantic eagles, which swooped down and bore them off. He remembered then to have heard of some distant valley where the diamond-collectors took this way to gather jewels they could not otherwise reach — the diamonds sticking fast in the flesh, and the eagles bearing all to their nests in the cliffs, where the merchants found them. Marco Polo, if I remember rightly, tells this story too.

Seeing how the case stood, Sindbad gathered a great package of the finest diamonds to be found —tied the package to his girdle in front ; then tied a round of beef to his girdle behind, and lay down flat, with his face to the ground. He trusted that some great eagle would lift him, and the meat, and diamonds, and all.

And there came a mammoth bird, — not so large as a roc, by any means, — but yet equal to the work. Slowly but surely, Sindbad was borne up by it from the earth — borne away to the cliffs, and dropped into a nest of young eaglets, where the diamond-searchers were in waiting to snatch the jewels.

You may be sure they were very much surprised to
see Sindbad, and were astonished when he showed them
the treasures in his package.   However, he gave them
a generous share, — visited their city, saw the king, — as
was usual for strangers, — and finally sailed away with
a rich load of jewels for home.   And this was the end
of his second voyage.

On his third voyage, this unlucky Sindbad was
wrecked again.   He saves his life, indeed, and with
a few of his comrades wanders upon the shores of a
strange country, where at last he enters the doors of
a great palace.   It must have been a rude palace; for
there were bones of men upon the floor, — fresh bones
too; and a great fire in the palace chimney-place, and
fearful-looking spits.   Sindbad and the men with him
crouched in the corner; and the walls around them
shook, as the master of the palace came stalking in.
He had a horrible figure.   If you have ever read
Homer, you must remember the great one-eyed Cyclop, who lived in a cavern, and devoured the companions of Ulysses.   Well, this monstrous creature, into
whose palace Sindbad had wandered, was one-eyed, like
the Cyclop, and far more hideous to look upon.   His
teeth were long and pointed, and his ears were like the
ears of an elephant, and flapped upon his shoulders.

You may be sure he saw these castaway sailors with
that great red eye of his; and presently coming up and
pinching one or two between his fingers, to find the fat-
test of them, he picked out one; then he lifted him
as a cook would lift a partridge, and thrust him through
with one of those cruel spits.   The sailors knew then
what the fire meant, and the men's bones; and I sus-

pect Sindbad must have been glad he was in so lean
condition; for he had been one of the first this monstrous creature had taken in hand.

Having eaten, the monster slept, — they generally
sleep pretty soundly, — though his snoring was something dreadful to listen to. Sindbad and the men with
him crept slily out from their corner, while the monster
slept; and, putting eight or nine of the iron spits in the
fire until they were well heated, thrust them all at once
into the one eye that was in the middle of the giant's
forehead. Then they all made for the shore with as
much haste as they could. They put together rafts out
of timbers lying there — dreading every moment lest
the blinded giant should find his way to them. They
finished their rafts, however, and had pushed off, when,
with a howling that echoed all along the shores, they
saw the giant striding toward them, — led by another,
and followed by some half-dozen others. In the Greek
story — as you will find when you come to read it —
there were only three of the Cyclops family — which
seems quite enough. This company of Eastern giants
did not reach the shore till Sindbad and his friends had
paddled a long way off: but they were not safe; for the
giants began pelting them with stones, and battered
their rafts in pieces. Somehow Sindbad saved himself
upon a log, and drifted into a far-away bay, where he
landed with one or two companions. He had a wonderful escape here from huge serpents, who devoured
the men with him; and, from a tall tree into which he
had climbed, he sees a ship off shore, and waves his
turban, and is seen, and is taken off, and carried to his
home again, — managing somehow to carry a great deal

of money back with him from this voyage, as he did from all the others.

He makes seven voyages in all, of which he tells the story in seven succeeding days, to that old porter Hindbad, of whom I spoke in the beginning. And he not only tells the stories to Hindbad; but he gives him a bag of golden coin every time he has finished a story of a voyage. I presume that Hindbad thought them very excellent stories, and would have dearly liked to hear more of them.

And he is not the only one who has thought them good. I cannot tell you the half of his wonderful adventures. Once, when cast away, he comes, with the sailors who were saved with him, upon another Roc's egg; which his companions — never having seen one before — commence hewing in pieces. In a moment the air is darkened; the great birds, whose nests these wanderers have disturbed, hang over them like a cloud; and when they would escape by taking to their boats, the birds, like the great Cyclops, take huge rocks, and sailing in the air above the ships, drop their burden, and make a wreck of the vessels.

That lucky Sindbad escapes, as he always manages to do; but in the new lands to which he is floated upon a piece of the wreck, he finds one of the strangest of all his adventures. The trees are beautiful, and the streams of water; there are sweet-smelling flowers too; and in this country, which seems as if it were altogether only a pleasant garden, he meets an old man, with long white beard, and deep-set prying eyes, limping along by the bank of a stream. Sindbad, at the beckoning of this droll-looking old man, takes him on his shoulders to help

The Old Man of the Sea.

him across the stream. But no sooner is he upon Sindbad's back than his legs seem to grow long, and cling
about the poor sailor, and his fingers stretch out into
claws that hold him fast ; and he settles to his place
upon Sindbad's shoulders as if he grew there. Sindbad
stoops for the old man to come down ; but the old man
does not come down : instead of it, he chuckles, and
gives Sindbad a punch in his ribs, and urges him to go
forward.

And forward this poor sailor of Bagdad is compelled
to go ; over hill and brook, and through valleys, and past
wide plains, — by noon, by night, — this terrible old Man
of the Sea keeps his place, and comes near to choking
Sindbad with the tightness of his hug. He makes Sindbad stay when he would pluck fruit from the trees ; he
warns him to go faster, when, through fatigue, he halts
and trembles under this terrible load.

Hindbad — being a porter — and used to carrying burdens on his shoulders, must have listened very wonder-
ingly to this story of a load which could not be shaken
off. Had it been a cask or a box, there would have been
more hope ; but a burden in the shape of a man is a
very hard thing to shake off.

And how was Sindbad rid of him at last ? Why, one
day (after he had carried the old man a week or more),
he saw some empty gourds lying on the ground ; and,
taking one of them, he pressed the juice — from some
of the delicious grapes that grew all around — into it, and
then hung his gourd upon a tree. The juice turned into
wine after some days, as grape-juice is very apt to do.
And when he came to drink it, — being faint with the
continual burden of that horrible Man of the Sea, —

the old man snuffed the wine, and beckoned to Sindbad to give him a taste of it. And he took another, and another, and another taste, — as wine-drinkers when once started are inclined to do, — until at last Sindbad felt the old man loosening his hold : and he lay down with him ; and the hold was loosened more and more, until the old man had fallen off from his shoulders in a drunken sleep. Then Sindbad seized whatever weapon he could find, — stones, I presume, — and made an end of his tormentor.

Sindbad does not say so in his story ; but I think this old Man of the Sea belonged to a dreadful tribe called Badd-Habbidtz, stray members of which are found very often in the East nowadays, and sometimes in the West. If you ever meet one, I advise you not to let him get settled down on your shoulders.

Sindbad prospers again when once he has shaken off this obstinate old man : he makes friends in that beautiful country ; gathers great cargoes of tea and spices, and sails back with new and richer stores than ever to the dear old City of Bagdad.

There he lived always afterward in a princely house (if we may believe those who made the pictures for the " Arabian Nights "), and was befriended by the Caliph Haroun al Raschid, who certainly lived and did a great many wonderful things — whatever may be true of the voyaging Sindbad and of the porter Hindbad.

Bagdad, too, was a real city, and is a city still. You will find it on your maps of Asia, lying a little eastward of the great sandy wastes of Arabia, upon the banks of the river Tigris, which is a branch of the river Euphrates, on which, as tradition says, once bloomed the Garden of Paradise.

Sindbad must have sailed on his great voyages down through the Tigris, — then through the Euphrates, and so out into the Persian Gulf. You can go there now by the same track over which Sindbad carried home his treasures. But I fear you would be disappointed in the city. You would find low houses and narrow streets, and a Turkish governor in red woollen cap in place of the great Caliph. You would find the palaces and grand temples and hanging gardens ruined, and only be reminded of the days of Arabian Nights by the blazing noonday heats, by the camels coming in with their burdens, by the waving palm-trees, and by the tomb, which is still standing, of the beautiful Zobeide, who was the favorite wife of the great Caliph.

Ruined Temple at Bagdad.

For my part, I am content to stay away from the Turkish city of Bagdad of to-day. I am sure that the sight of its outlying valleys — whatever herds of sheep and cattle might be feeding on them — would not be equal to the image I have in mind when I read the Vision of Mirza ;[1] and in the city itself, I am quite sure that I should miss the great stretch of brilliant streets —

[1] I counsel all my young readers to find and read the delightful paper of Addison's in the Spectator, with this title.

the jewelled palaces — the troops of laden camels — the flashing cimeters — the rustle of silks — the fair Persians — the veiled princesses — the Shahs and Schahriars — the delightful Zobeides, — which come into my thought when I read the "Arabian-Nights" stories of the times of the magnificent Haroun al Raschid.

IV.

GOLDSMITH'S WORK.

A Vicar and his Family.

WHO, pray, has not read that delightful old story
about a certain Dr. Primrose, who was Vicar
of Wakefield? Was it in the Sunday-school library
that we first came upon it? — or was it on the book-
shelves of some darling old aunt who kept it as one of
the treasures of her school-days? For it is an old book :
our grandmothers read it, and may-be our great-grand-
mothers ; and I think it is quite certain that our grand-
children will read it too.

There are skipping-places in it, to be sure ; such are
some of the long talks about second marriages, which
don't concern young people much ; and such is the page-
long speech about kings and republics and free government : but with these taken out, or skipped over, — as
well as the Greek, which has no business there, — what
a delightful story it is !

One grows into the kindliest sort of companionship
with the good Dr. Primrose and his family, and follows

their fortunes as if they were fortunes of his own, and never forgets them, — let him live as long as he may.

Naturally we don't think as much of Mrs. Primrose as we do of the Doctor; but that happens in a good many families where we love to go. She is a little too proud of her daughters, — who are fine girls, both of them, — and a little too much bent upon holding up her head in the world.

Mrs. Primrose's Fine Girls.

Of course it is a very good thing to hold up one's head, and better still to be able to do so with a clear conscience; but we don't like to encounter people who want to impress everybody they meet — with a notion of their great importance. There was a little of this in Mrs. Primrose, but not a bit of it in the Doctor.

He was of good fortune when the story opens; and besides those two daughters, Sophia and Olivia, had two sons, George and Moses, as well as a couple of younger boys, who don't have much to do with the story; and for aught that appears, they may be young boys somewhere in England still.

Not much happens to interest one while the Doctor is comfortably rich. He says himself, that the most important event of a twelvemonth was the moving from the blue chamber to the brown ; that surely would not concern young fellows who have no moving to do. The son George does, indeed, fall in love with a very nice girl, — Miss Wilmot, who has a snug fortune of her own ; and as Miss Wilmot has a strong fancy for George, it is counted a settled thing between them ; and, indeed, the marriage-day was fixed.

But Dr. Primrose (I call him Doctor because Mr. Jenkinson, an important character in the story, always did, and I am sure if he had lived among our American colleges he would have been a doctor) — Dr. Primrose, I say, could not get over his love for talk about the wickedness of second marriages, in which Mr. Wilmot, the father of the charming Arabella, did not agree with him ; and as they waxed warm one day, Mr. Wilmot — I dare say, getting the worst of the argument — let slip the fact that the Doctor was a beggar, — since the business man who had been intrusted with his property had become bankrupt, and had fled from the country.

This was an ugly thing for Mr. Wilmot to say, and a rough way of pushing his cause ; but it was none the less true. And this fact and the quarrel broke off the match ; and son George, in high dudgeon, set off to seek his fortune otherwheres.

Nor was this the worst : the good Doctor had to leave his fine house, and take a poor parish in a distant part of the country, with a cottage so small that there could be no moving every spring from the blue chamber to the brown. There were no chambers to move into. But out of this change of home, and the griefs and trials that came with it, grew all those events which have made the history of the old Vicar so charming a one that it has been conned and read in ten thousand households all over the world.

Can I tell you what those events were in a half-hour of talk?

Ah, well! it will be spoiling one of the tenderest of stories; and yet I will try to catch so much of the pith and of the point of it as shall make you eager to taste for yourself, and "at first hands," the delicate humor and the charming flow of that old-fashioned novel of the Vicar of Wakefield. I call it a novel, though it is as unlike as possible to the work that our modern novel-writers do.

Mr. Burchell and the Squire.

Mrs. Primrose — poor woman — who had loved to put on airs in her large house, did not get over the love in the small house. It is a love that it is hard for anybody to get over, if they begin once to encourage it. But the Doctor, good soul, laughed at her grand dressing and her eagerness to show off her daughters in the old finery. She even aims at something like style in going to church, by rigging up the two plough-horses so that one should carry the boy Moses and herself with the two little ones, and the other make a mount for the two daughters. Of course it was but a sorry figure they cut, and the Doctor had his laugh at them, though it was on a Sunday. Yet when a middle-aged woman has an eye for "style," it is not easy to laugh her out of it; and

Mrs. Primrose was set on to this and a good many other like manœuvres by a hope she had of making conquest of a certain Squire Thornhill, — who was their landlord and the great man of the neighborhood, — and of matching him with one of her daughters. He was of fair age, lived freely in a grand house, rode to the hounds, and sent presents of game to the Primrose girls, — much to

Mrs. Primrose's "Style."

the delight of their mamma ; who banters Olivia specially on these attentions, and wonders the Doctor — simple soul — cannot see through it all. She has even hopes of capturing the Squire's chaplain — or the man who passes as chaplain — for her daughter Sophia ; who is a sweeter girl than Olivia, — though not so coquettish and not taking so much after the mother.

They say in the neighborhood that Squire Thornhill is indebted for his easy way of living to the bounty of an eccentric uncle, — not much older than himself, but more grave, living much in London, not well known down in the country, but spoken of always with very much awe.

The Primrose family, moreover, make the acquaintance of a Mr. Burchell, — whom they meet first, I think, upon the highway; and who does good service by saving Sophia from drowning, when she had fallen, one day, into the river that ran near by. He is a shabby-genteel person in appearance, but well instructed, and can talk by the hour with the Doctor about his hobbies; and he brings little gifts for the boys; indeed, if he had been rich and better-looking, Mrs. Primrose would have been half-disposed to favor him as a proper match for Sophia — provided the chaplain should fail her.

A curious thing is, that Mr. Burchell doesn't talk in the highest terms of Squire Thornhill; and another curious thing is, that he avoids any occasion of meeting him at the Vicar's cottage — all which Madame Primrose places to the account of the poor man's jealousy. Maybe so; but the Doctor thought well of him and of his talk, and so did Moses and the boys; and it always seemed to me that Sophia — though she never said so — looked kindly on him, and was not so much disturbed by his lack of fine clothes as Olivia or her mother.

They were all flustered and provoked, however, when they learned, in an accidental way, that Burchell, by some talk and letters of his, had prevented the two girls from carrying out a plan they had formed of going up to London with a couple of lady friends of Squire

Thornhill's. These town ladies had been down to the country, and paid a visit to the Vicarage, very much to the delight of Madame Primrose, who could never have done with admiring their fine feathers and silks. It would be a splendid thing for the dear girls to go up to London with them !

The Doctor did not, indeed, think quite so highly of these town ladies ; but what business had Mr. Burchell to interfere, and by his misrepresentations to defeat what would have been such a pleasure to the girls? 'Twas a shabby intermeddling in his family affairs ; and he told Mr. Burchell so with some warmth. And Mr. Burchell was warm too ; and what business had the Doctor to be prying into the contents of private letters of his? In short, they made a sharp family quarrel of it with Mr. Burchell, and Burchell took his stick and walked away. This was the last they saw of him for a long time.

Did Sophia possibly look after him with a little yearning and repenting? I used to ask myself that question when I read the story in my young days ; but I don't think she did — certainly not at the moment.

Well, the Doctor's money affairs were not getting on well : I think Madame Primrose and her love for good style had something to do with it. Good style, as it is called, has very much to do then, and always, with — not getting on well.

The good folks of the family had sent Moses off to the Fair to make sale of the colt ; but Moses was horri- bly cheated, and came back with only a gross of green spectacles — of which, you may be sure, he never heard the last. The good Doctor thought to mend matters by taking the only remaining horse himself. The rogues would never cheat *him:* but they did, and very badly too; for he brought back only a worthless bit of paper, which was a draft on Neighbor Flamborough, who had two bouncing daughters, — one of whom Moses was tender upon. The Vicar had taken this draft from the man Jenkinson, who had talked Greek with the Doctor, and praised a book he had written, and so made the good man believe that he, — Jenkinson, was the worthiest and most benevolent creature in the world.

Moses had the laugh now. But it was no laughing time for the family: they were growing poorer and poorer. Mrs. Primrose's "style" was getting uncomfortably pinched; and the match with the Squire didn't get on: so she thought to spur his attentions by setting up a new claimant for Miss Olivia, in Farmer Williams, who lived hard by. This had not gone very far, when, one day, the boys ran in, crying out, — "Olivia is gone!"

And so she had — in a coach: it was a runaway of a very bad kind. Was Burchell the criminal, or who? The old gentleman seized his pistols, and would have made after the wretch, but his wife and poor weeping Sophy quieted him.

It came out shortly after, that Thornhill was the man; and that he had made a mock marriage, and had made two or three such before. And yet the villain had the daring to call upon the Doctor with explanations; but the good man blazed upon him with all the rage of injured innocence. The Squire was cool; for Dr. Primrose owed him large debts, which there was no means of paying.

Olivia found her way back, broken-hearted, and was

warmly greeted by the father, though she met only a
half-welcome from Mrs. Primrose.

It came to a prison, at last, for the good Vicar ; for in
those days people who could not or would not pay their
debts were clapped into prisons. The family of the
good man would not leave him, but journeyed up to the
town where the jail lay — though it was winter weather,
the ground covered in snow, and poor Olivia just recov-

Going to Prison.

ering from a slow fever. The parishioners of the Doctor
would, indeed, have snatched him from the keeping of
the officers of the law, as they set out on their journey ;
but the good Vicar in his earnest way checked them, and
bade them remember that without law there could be no
justice, and they must respect what the law commanded.

What Happened in Prison.

For a long time Dr. Primrose lay in that dreary jail; his family paying him frequent visits, and he by kindly talk winning upon the company of his fellow-prisoners — among whom happened to be that very Jenkinson who had so deceived him on his visit to the horse-fair, but who now at last seemed repentant.

Surely it was a very sorry time for the poor Primrose family : the father in prison for debts he could find no means to pay ; the oldest son a wanderer — none knew where ; Olivia a poor disgraced creature ; and to add to the sum of troubles, it is reported that the lawless Squire Thornhill is to marry the charming Miss Wilmot, who had been once the promised bride of the poor wandering George Primrose. This seemed enough to break down all faith in that Providence whose overwatching care the good Vicar had always preached. Yet still further griefs were in store : Sophia — poor Sophia — in one of her walks into the country, where she hoped to catch some new strength and bloom, was stolen away — gone, none knew whither. And, as if to crown all, the wandering vagabond George returns — not with honors, but a prisoner, with shackles upon his limbs. He has heard of the wrong done his poor sister Olivia ; in his anger, he has challenged Squire Thornhill to mortal combat ; he has resisted the servants of that base master, — has cut one down with his sword.

Indeed, it is a sorry group in that prison : the son a felon ; the Doctor a hopeless debtor ; Olivia disgraced and broken-hearted ; Sophia gone !

That was the place in this old story for tears — if anybody had them; and a good many did have them; and I have no doubt will have them in years to come. But we fellows didn't stop there — for all the crying. We felt sure something better was to happen. And it did, — it did.

First of all, Sophia was brought back, rescued; and who do you think brought her back? Why, Mr. Burchell, — old seedy Burchell; and the family — even to Mrs. Primrose — cannot help thanking the man, notwithstanding his shabby clothes.

Mr. Jenkinson, too, proves a friend at last — is ready to swear that the marriage of Olivia to Squire Thornhill was not a mock marriage at all, but a real marriage; for he himself had brought the priest who went through the ceremony.

The good Doctor was enraptured at this; and Mrs. Primrose went up and kissed poor, shrinking Olivia — for the first time. (I never liked Mrs. Primrose overmuch.)

After this, Miss Arabella Wilmot comes in to see the poor Vicar, and is much taken aback to find George there: she blushes, and is disturbed; for, to tell truth, she has never loved any one else; and when occasion permitted, I dare say she told him so; for they were hand in hand, in a corner, before much time had passed.

Squire Thornhill came in, — for what reason I don't know exactly, — but got hard looks from everybody; most of all from Mr. Burchell, whom he seemed to fear greatly.

Can you fancy why he should? — It was all clear enough presently; for this Mr. Burchell — old, seedy

Burchell — was none other than the famous and wealthy and eccentric Sir William Thornhill, on whose favor the reckless young squire was dependent. However, the uncle let his nephew off easily, but compelled him to acknowledge publicly his marriage with Miss Olivia.

Then came old father Wilmot, with the story that the man of business who had run away with the Vicar's fortune had been captured, and there was good chance that all his property would be restored. George, too, would be cleared from imprisonment: at least, Sir William Thornhill said he would bring it about; and nobody doubted that he would.

Of course the Primrose family had now reason to be happy; and they all looked so except Sophia, who wore a very sad countenance. The truth is, when Mr. Burchell had brought her back to her father, the good Doctor — knowing her preserver only as Mr. Burchell — had told him in his gratitude, that, as he had rescued her, he deserved to possess her, — to which Mr. Burchell had not made much reply.

But now Mr. Burchell — that is, Sir William Thornhill, — with all the dignity that should belong to a great baronet, said that he was glad to see prosperity restored to this Primrose family; — that he had a great respect for the good Doctor (he didn't say any thing about Mrs. Primrose); — that he was glad to see so many happy faces about him, and that the only exceptions were the faces of Miss Sophia and Mr. Jenkinson. He thought Jenkinson deserved well of the Vicar; and he proposed that the good man should give Sophia to him as a bride, and he himself, he said, would add a wedding portion of five hundred pounds.

But Sophia's face did not clear up at all : nay, there were angry tears in her eyes as she vowed with a pitiful, low voice — that she would not have Mr. Jenkinson at all, — *never!*

"Why, then," said Sir William Thornhill, "I must take the dear girl myself ;" and with that he snatched her to his arms.

Could there be a prettier ending to that story of the Primroses ? No wonder it charmed us ; no wonder it has charmed thousands.

And what became of Moses? Why, Moses married one of the bouncing Miss Flamboroughs, of course. And I'll warrant you that Mrs. Primrose let everybody know, within twenty miles round, that her daughter became Lady Thornhill ; and I will warrant further, that Sir William never took to his mother-in-law very strongly, and never enjoyed her gooseberry-wine so much — as when he drank it outside her own house.

Poor Goldy.

And was there really a Dr. Primrose who told this story about his own family, and about the vanities of his wife, and who married his daughter to Mr. Burchell — otherwise known as Sir William Thornhill ?

No — no — no !

It is as little true of any one, as that Master Aladdin found a lamp which worked the wonders we read of in the chapter that went before this.

The person who really told this story of Dr. Primrose was an Irishman, of the name of Goldsmith, who used to be talked of among those who knew him best as "poor Goldy." He was a short, thick-set man, marked with old traces of small-pox, with a quick, clear black eye, and head almost bald.

Among his friends was the famous painter Sir Joshua Reynolds, who made a picture of him, from which most of the engravings are made, and which I am sure was not a little flattered. I give it to you here.

Leslie, the painter, said he saw in it all the genius that went to the "Vicar of Wakefield," and the "Deserted Village;" and I dare say Sir Joshua Reynolds painted it (as he should have done) with the memory of all the best things poor Goldy had done, quickening his skill, and lightening up his touches on the canvas. Without this knowing and feeling of a man's inner life, good portraits are never made.

I said that Goldsmith was nearly bald-headed, and he so appears in Reynolds's picture; but it was the custom of that day — the latter part of the last century — to wear wigs; and Goldsmith almost always wore a wig.

Bunbury's Goldsmith

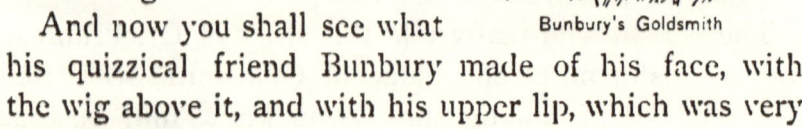

And now you shall see what his quizzical friend Bunbury made of his face, with the wig above it, and with his upper lip, which was very

protruding, making a show that must have provoked
Goldsmith; yet it was said to be very like him. He
played a great many games of cards with his friend
Bunbury, — of which game he was always over-fond;
but I think he would never have forgiven that friend
if he had known that we now, more than a century later,
should be looking at it, and calling it a fair picture
of him.

As he loved cards and gaming, so he loved wine overmuch, and was often the worse for it. I don't mean to
say that he went so far as to make a sot of himself, but
that he lingered often and often over tavern-tables when
he might have been doing better things. And remember
in excuse for him, that he lived in days when almost
everybody drank wine in taverns, and when even that
great man Dr. Johnson — who was also a friend of Goldsmith's — sometimes drank so much as to forget himself,
and to make his great figure reel along the walk on the
way to his chambers.

Dr. Johnson was the great literary character of that
day (it was in the reign of George II. and George
III.), and wrote the best Dictionary of the English Language — until Dr. Webster made a better one; and it
was through this very Dr. Sam Johnson, that the
story of Dr. Primrose, I have told you of, found its way
first to the printer's hands.

You would like to know how it happened; and it is a
thing you ought to know. Well — one day, Dr. Johnson,
being at dinner with Mrs. Thrale, who was a great friend
of Johnson's, received a message from poor Goldy, saying that he was in distress, and "would the Doctor call
round and see him?"

Goldy was living, at that time, in Wine-Office Court, near Fleet Street; and there the Doctor went to see him, having sent a guinea by the messenger to relieve any pressing trouble. Goldy had used the guinea to buy (among other things) a bottle of wine, and was sitting over it when the Doctor came in.

Goldsmith's Lodgings.

" I put the cork in the bottle," says the Doctor, "and begged him to be calm." Then he learned that his landlady was threatening him for his rent, and that the sheriffs were ready to pounce upon him. He took a manuscript from his drawer, and begged the Doctor to sell it for him. This was the Vicar of Wakefield — that delightful old story of which I have given you a glimpse.

Dr. Johnson, seeing it had merit, — but not, I think, seeing all its merit — (for it is not much like Rasselas,

which was a story by Dr. Johnson, that it may be worth
your while to read) went out with it, and sold it for sixty
pounds.

The bookseller who bought it thought so little of it,
that the story lay in his drawer for fifteen months before
it was given to the printer. It appeared finally in 1766,
when Goldsmith was thirty-eight years old. The critics
did not speak very well of the book at the first : some
of them thought it worth their while to make fun of the
Primrose family ; but it grew steadily in favor, month
by month and year by year, and is now read all over the
world.

A great German, who was young when it first appeared, hit upon the tale some four years after, and read
it with delight and admiration ; and seventy years later,
when he read it again with renewed delight, he told a
friend how much its first reading had to do with forming
his education. This great German was Goethe.

We told you that Goldsmith was in distress when he
wrote the Vicar of Wakefield, and beset by poverty.
He never outlived that sort of distress ; for though the
booksellers have received thousands and thousands of
pounds for that little book, only the first paltry sixty
pounds ever went into the pockets of the author.

I do not think he would ever have been rich, if he had
received thousands for it. He never had the art of
husbanding his moneys, and never knew how to spend
them with judgment. His heart was easily touched by
any story of suffering ; and he would give his last guinea
to a begging woman in the street. He loved dearly,
too, a good roistering tavern supper, where he could lift
up his voice to a great roar of song ; and he paid for a

great many such suppers, from which richer men than he slunk away, and left him to the "reckoning." He had a passion for gaming, too, — or, as we should say — gambling, of which I have already spoken. But, before we condemn him too much for this, let us remember that in that day, and in London, gambling was common in most of the respectable houses; and the great orator Charles James Fox would lose, and did lose, as much as eleven thousand pounds at a single sitting.

Another fancy — and a queer one — of poor Goldy's, was his passion for dress. Looking back at Bunbury's picture of him, you would never imagine that he should have a love for silk waistcoats, and velvet breeches, and ruffles, and plush coats. Yet nothing is more true; and there are old bills of his still in existence, in which are set down in fair figures — and very long ones — what he paid for "Ratteen surtout," and "Blue Velvet Suit," and "Silk breeches," and "Queen's blue dress suit," and "Princess stuff breeches."

Yet he was not — as we should say — a society man. He knew few ladies; he never married — never was near marrying. I cannot find, by any hint, that he ever loved any young woman better than any old one; or that any young woman ever loved him tenderly. Indeed, his appearance could never have been very engaging; and his manner in a mixed company was always somewhat clownish.

Mr. Boswell, who was a member of the same club with him, and a great friend of Dr. Johnson's (whose biography he wrote), was much more of a society man, and much less of a man in every other way. He used to sneer at "poor Goldy" and his over-fine clothes; and I

think would never have been seen in the street with
him, except that the great Dr. Johnson befriended Goldsmith, and patted him, in his bear-like way, upon the
back.

His Family and Death.

I have said that no Dr. Primrose ever *really* lived;
but there were those who said that Goldsmith's old
father, who had been a clergyman in Ireland, and who
died when the son was quite young, was in many things
very like to Dr. Primrose.

It was almost in the middle of Ireland that Goldsmith
was born, — not far from Roscommon, and very near to
Edgeworthtown — where lived, later, that good woman
Maria Edgeworth, whom you also know by her stories,
and to whose acquaintance I shall introduce you in a
coming chapter of this little book.

He has not the best of schooling in that little village,
nor has the poor parish priest — his father — much
money to spare. Later, the old gentleman gets a larger
and richer parish, — just as Dr. Primrose did not, — and
Oliver has a better chance. But he loves to make a
song for village idlers, and to hear them roar it out at
a tavern table, — better than to study.

And, after his father's death, he becomes more of
a vagrant; sometimes studying; sometimes tutoring;
sometimes trading horses, — always selling one for less
than he is worth, and always buying one for more than
he is worth — as most people do. He has some bicker-
ings with his mother, too, — who does not like vagrancy.

At one time he goes away to Cork, and actually

engages place on a ship for America; but this plan
gets somehow upset. If he had come! Do you think
he would have written a "Deserted Village" and a
"Vicar of Wakefield" over here? Or would he have
slipped into practical ways, and taught the violin, or
kept a country tavern, or had an office in the Custom
House?

On one of his jaunts about the Irish country, he found
himself belated one night in a village far from home;
and, inquiring after a public house, some wag directed
him to a gentleman's place, where Goldy went, — and
ordered out his horse, — and fumed, — and put on important airs, — and wanted the best supper that could
be had; and did not find out that he was making free
with the home of a private gentleman until he asked
for his bill next morning. Out of this little adventure
grew afterward that charming play of "She Stoops to
Conquer," which you may see now, from time to time,
upon the stage; and which is better worth seeing than
most of the comedies of to-day.

By the help of a rich uncle, he gets a footing afterward at college; later he goes to study medicine at
Edinboro'; and thence he goes over — sent by the same
good uncle — to Leyden in Holland, where was a famous
university.

Who knows but he might have made a great Doctor,
if he had kept by his chances there? But he doesn't:
we presently find him wandering about Europe — sleeping in stables, in religious houses, in small inns — paying his way sometimes by the music he made with the
flute he took with him; and perhaps it was over-use of
this that made that great upper lip of his project so
much as you see it does in Bunbury's caricature.

I suppose nobody ever went through Europe, seeing so much, with so little money, as Goldsmith. You will see traces of this wandering in his poem of the "Traveller;" and here and there in the "Bee,"—which was another of his books; and most of all, in the wanderings of George Primrose, in the "Vicar."

Coming to London again, he tried medicine, with velvet coats and big wig to help him; but he never did much at medicine. He tried teaching; but he was not steady enough and patient enough to get on well at this. Then he became proof-reader—that is to say,—he corrected the printed sheets for Dr. Richardson, a bookseller, who had written novels—one of which, called "Clarissa," was thought superb, and everybody read it. Women would go a block out of their way to see the dear and famous Dr. Richardson. And now scarce anybody knows about "Clarissa;" but all the world knows the "Vicar."

After this, he kept by books; writing some which brought him more money than the Primrose story, but not nearly so well known now. He wrote so well that

Goldy, Johnson, and Boswell.

he was asked to join the club,—a very famous club, where he used to meet Burke (another great Irishman and an orator), and Beauclerc, and Boswell, and Dr. Johnson, and Sir Joshua Reynolds, and Garrick the great actor. With some one or two of these, he might

have been seen over and over in those times, walking
along Fleet Street in London.

They all liked him ; and there were times when they
all laughed at him. He never would have made a Mr.
Worldly-Wiseman, such as comes into Bunyan's story of
the Pilgrim. He was always at "sixes and sevens."
He was petulant in his talk often, and he had vanities
that crept into his manner ; but his vices were such as
disposed one more to laugh than to be shocked by
them. And in all he wrote, he was so simple, and pure,
and healthy, and withal there was such play of delightful
humor, and all of his stories were so tenderly told, that
people loved him for his books, and keep on loving him
for them to-day.

Poor and lonely in his chamber, he only knew cheer
when he was with some favorite member of the club, or
with some humble companion at a coffee-room table.
Poor and lonely he died ; with few friends about him,
— neither mother, nor wife, nor brother, nor sister near
him when his great black eye grew dim, and the light of
it passed away forever.

The great statesman Edmund Burke, when the tid-
ings of the death came to him, burst into tears. Sir
Joshua Reynolds, when the messenger came to say
Goldy was dead — laid his brushes down — shut up his
studio, and gave the day up to his grief. Burly old
Dr. Johnson was touched keenly, and mourned his death
as he had mourned for very few.

They buried him in tne Temple Church-yard, quietly ;
but among the mourners were men so highly and so
worthily known, that the presence of one of them was
worth more to the fame and memory of poor Goldy than

would have been the presence of a host of gilded carriages, and the blaze of idle ceremony.

There is a tablet in honor of this writer of the Primrose story, in Westminster Abbey; and upon it a Latin inscription — by Dr. Johnson, with one line in it, I dare say you have seen somewhere : —

Nullum quod tetigit non ornavit.

It was so aptly said, that it has been said of many others since; but never said so truly as of poor Goldy.

No one knows just where he lies buried in Temple Church-yard, for there is no record. But they have placed a stone with his name upon it on the north side of the Temple Church, a little west of the master's house; and there visitors go every Sunday — strangers from all countries — men, and women, and children, to see the stone which bears the name of the man who told such a winning story of a poor Vicar and his family.

He will never be forgotten. He deserves to be remembered.

V.

GULLIVER SWIFT.

Some Queer Little People.

A HUNDRED and fifty years ago, or thereabout, while George the First was King of Great Britain, there was a story of some voyages printed in England, which everybody read with a great deal of wonder.

There never had been such voyages made before; there never had been such people seen as this voyager had seen.

A man who said his name was Richard Sympson sent the story of these voyages to the printer or publisher, and told him, and told the public, that *he* knew the man who wrote the story, and that he was living in Nottinghamshire in England, and that he was a friend of his, and connected with him on the mother's side. And, besides this, he said that he was a truthful man, and that his neighbors believed what he said. He knew the house in which he had lived, too, and knew who his father was — which was not very strange, since he was connected with him, as I said, on the mother's side.

The name of this voyager was Lemuel Gulliver; and he was so much thought of among his neighbors (Mr. Sympson said), that it came to be a proverb among them, when any one told a thing that was very, *very* true, to add, — " It's as true as if Mr. Gulliver had said it."

Well, this Mr. Gulliver said he studied physic in Leyden, and married Mary Burton, who lived in Newgate Street, and that he got four hundred pounds in money by his wife. I don't see any reason to doubt this. He went as surgeon on a good many ships ; but nothing happened to him very extraordinary, until he sailed in May, 1699, in the "Antelope," for the South Seas. (I knew a ship, once, called the "Antelope.") This "Antelope" was commanded by Capt. William Prichard ; but that doesn't matter much, since Mr. Gulliver doesn't refer to Capt. Prichard once again.

They had a very hard time of it, — a good many of the sailors dying off ; and on the 5th of November — a little while before Thanksgiving Day in New England — the ship drove on a rock, and split.

Ships do so very often when they drive on rocks.

Six of the men got clear, with Gulliver, and rowed until the wind upset the boat. The six men were drowned ; but Gulliver touched bottom, and walked a mile through the water till he reached land. Then being very tired, and, as he says, "having taken half a pint of brandy aboard ship," he was very sleepy, and lay down to doze. This about the brandy is, I dare say, not more than half true.

He says he must have slept about nine hours, and when he waked he felt stiff, and couldn't turn over. He

tried to lift his arm, but he couldn't. Presently he
found out that there was a cord across his breast, and
another across the middle of his body; and then he
found that his legs were tied, and his arms; and it
seemed to him — though he couldn't tell certainly —
that his hair was fastened to the ground. This was all
strange enough; but it was stranger yet when he felt
something walk up over his left leg, and come on across

Six Inches High.

his body, almost to his chin, so that by turning his eyes
down, he could see a little fellow, about six inches high,
formed just like a man, with a bow and arrows in his
hand. One would have been enough; but when he felt
forty more walking over his legs and arms, and pulling
themselves up by his hair, he roared out, — as I think
you and I would have done.

Gulliver on Exhibition.

At this they all scampered; and some of them hurt themselves badly by tumbling off his body, though this Mr. Gulliver did not know until some time afterward. The poor voyager, who was thus lying on his back, struggled a little, and so he came to get his left arm loose; which was very lucky for him, because these little people, who were much frightened, began to shoot arrows at him, and would most certainly have put out his eyes if he had not covered them with his hand.

But, by little and little, he was able to look about him, and saw there thousands and thousands of these queer small people in the fields around.

Afterward, when he had made signs that he was hungry and thirsty, they brought him food, a wagon-load at a time, which he took up between his thumb and finger; and their casks of wine, — no bigger than a tea-cup, — he emptied in a way that made them wonder. (Of course, if these people were only six inches high, their wine-casks must have been small in proportion; every one must see the truth of that.) But these little people had put drugs in the wine, so that Mr. Gulliver slept very soundly after it, — so soundly that he didn't know at all when they brought an immense cart or truck (which they used for dragging vessels), and slung him upon it; and with fifteen hundred of the king's horses drew him to town. There they chained him by one leg, near to the entrance of an immense temple, with a door four feet high — so that he was able to crawl under cover when he awoke.

Of course all the little people round about came to see Mr. Gulliver, whom they called "The Man-Mountain;" and the king, who had a majestic figure, since he

was taller by half an inch than any of his subjects,
appointed officers to show the Man-Mountain, and the
officers in this way made a great deal of money out of
Mr. Gulliver.   Officers almost always make money out
of somebody.

He caught their language, after a time ; though they
couldn't have spoken louder than our crickets — if as
loud.   The name of this strange country was Liliput ;
and Mr. Gulliver was introduced to all the distinguished
people there, — at least he says so, — and has a good
deal to say about the queen and the princesses, and how
he amused them.   Travellers are apt to.   He helped
them, too, very much ; and when a people living upon a
neighboring island called Blefuscu threatened war, and
collected a great fleet of vessels to attack the Liliputians, Mr. Gulliver kindly waded over one morning, and,
tying a cord to all the ships' bows, drew them along
after him, and gave them up to his imperial majesty of
Liliput.   He had to put on his spectacles, however,
while he was in the water, to keep the Blefuscan
soldiers — who were collected on the shores by thousands — from shooting out his eyes.

The King of Liliput was, of course, delighted with
this service of Mr. Gulliver, and made him a prince on
the spot.   He also thought it would be a good thing if
Mr. Gulliver should, some day, wade across again, and
drag over the rest of the enemy's ships ; but the Englishman did not think very well of this, and I suspect
this difference led to a little coolness between him and
the king.   It is certain that a good many of the high
officers took up a dislike of Mr. Gulliver, as well as some
of the ladies of the court.   The long and the short of it

was, that he found himself out of place among the Liliputians, and so went over afoot to the island of Blefuscu,
where he soon was on very good terms with the emperor
of that empire, though he had drawn away his ships.

One day, however, Mr. Gulliver espied in the offing an
English boat bottom side up, and by dint of wading and
tugging, with the aid of several Blefuscan men-of-war, he
brought it to land. There he repaired the boat, — the
emperor kindly consenting, and furnishing a few hundred mechanics to aid him. Then he stocked the boat
with provisions, taking some live sheep and cattle, and
set off homeward. He ran great danger of being
wrecked; but, finally fell in with an English merchant
vessel, — Capt. John Biddel, commander, — who kindly
took him on board, and asked him how he happened to
be at sea in a yawl?

Mr. Gulliver told him, and described the people he
had been with. Capt. Biddel didn't believe him, and
thought him crazy. Whereupon Mr. Gulliver pulled
some of the Blefuscan sheep and cattle out of his pocket,
and showed them to him.

Capt. Biddel couldn't say any thing more. Mr. Gulliver arrived home safely; found his wife well, and his
boy Johnny (named after his uncle, who had left him
some land at Epping) at the grammar school.

Some Monstrous People.

This same Mr. Gulliver made three or four more
voyages, and always had the luck to fall in with most
extraordinary people, — some of them being ninety feet

high; and he was for a considerable time in the waist-
coat pocket of a farmer.

Only imagine what the wheat must have been, and the
pumpkins, and the green corn — where a farmer could
quietly put a great traveller like Mr. Gulliver in his
vest-pocket! People get into farmers' pockets in this
country, — but not in that way.

The potatoes in that land of Brobdingnag (for so the
country was called) must have come up to Mr. Gulliver's
waistband; and as for the potato plants, they would
have made a great craggy forest over his head; and the
Colorado beetles (which probably did not live in that
time) would have been huge creatures, upon whose back
a man might ride.

Think, too, of what the trees must have been in such
a region: the great California Red-woods would have
been mere walking-sticks; and the mountains would
have risen up at least some sixty or seventy miles in the
air, and of course would have been seen a very long distance away. Just what that distance might be, looking
over the sea, it will be easy for you to calculate.

It seems very strange that a land with such huge
mountains upon it should never have been discovered
until Mr. Lemuel Gulliver passed that way; and yet
this is hardly more strange than the other things he
tells.

One would have thought that such monstrous people
with their monstrous tools of all kinds — a sickle was
larger than our scythes — should have had great tele-
scopes too, so that wonderful sights would be opened to
them in the skies; but if it were so, he tells us nothing
of it. On another of his voyages, however, to a land

called Laputa, — which was a land that floated about in the air and was directed by a huge magnet, — he does tell us of strange things discovered in the sky. Among the rest, he assures us that these Laputans had found out that the planet Mars had two moons or satellites revolving about it, — whereof one revolves in the space of ten hours, and the other in twenty-one and a half.

You may be sure that the British astronomers had no faith in this when Gulliver reported it; certainly no one except these Laputans had ever seen such moons: and now, in this year 1877, it proves that the report is quite true, and that there are such moons, — though their times of revolution may be a little different, — and they have been discovered through the great telescope in Washington.

What if the other reports which Gulliver made should some day prove to be true! What if we should find somewhere in the interior of Africa queer little people like Liliputians, or great monsters of men like those of Brobdingnag!

Though these last were monstrous in size, they were excellent, quiet people. Gulliver had a great many long talks with their King, who had a strong liking for this little traveller, and led him on to tell all about the government and usages of the country from which he had sailed. He thought Mr. Gulliver did a wise thing in sailing away from it. For when he heard of the bickering, and wars, and bribery, and cheating, and prisons, which were common in England, he thought the people must be "contemptible little vermin," and said so plainly to Mr. Gulliver.

Mr. Gulliver does not seem to have been offended, or

at least he did not resent this plain talking; and when
he told the King further, that in his country men were
used to making great tubes of metal (as large as his
majesty's tooth-pick), and filled them with a black powder
and hot shot, and then fired them off with a terrible
explosion, so as to kill and maim as many men as possible at one blast — the big King was horrified. And,
when one thinks of it closely, it does seem horrible.

Gulliver told the King, one day, in the course of a conversation, which he held by sitting upon a chair placed
on a cabinet, and the cabinet on a table, — all which
brought Mr. Gulliver about on a level with the King's
ear, who kindly took a low seat, — I say Gulliver told
the King that in his country — meaning England —
there were a thousand works published on the art of
government. The big King said only, "Pooh! pooh!"
but afterward gave it as his opinion that "whoever
could make two ears of corn or two blades of grass to
grow upon a spot of ground where only one grew before,
would deserve better of mankind, and do more service to
his country, than the whole race of politicians put
together."

A good many orators have said the same thing since;
but the King of Brobdingnag said it first.

Of course Mr. Gulliver must have found it very awk
ward in getting about in houses where the steps were all
five feet high, and where the level of the seats was sixteen feet above the floor. The flies, too, were as large
as robins, and came buzzing frightfully about his ears.
He had a very narrow escape, also, from a couple of
rats; when his great presence of mind alone saved him
from death.

It happened in this wise. He had been left asleep on a bedstead twenty feet from the floor, in a chamber which was about three hundred feet wide by five hundred feet long, and high in proportion. Waking up suddenly, he saw two enormous beasts, as large as large mastiffs, but with the whiskers and tails of rats, tramping toward him. One seized him by the collar, and had nearly throttled him, when he managed to draw out the short sword which he always wore, and with it he pierced the

Gulliver Kills a Rat.

monster rat through the body. The other ran away frightened, but not until the traveller had given him two or three good thwacks with his weapon.

He was, however, very limp and exhausted after this battle — as you observe in this picture of him.

Fortunately, Mr. Gulliver kept a journal, or else wrote

out the account of his travels and of his adventures
when they were fresh in his mind. But his friend Mr.
Sympson, of whom I spoke in the beginning, did not
cause his travels to be printed until a good many years
after. Why, I'm sure I don't know. When they *were*
printed, people in England were very much astonished;
and some curious ones went so far as to go down into
Nottinghamshire to have an interview with Mr. Gulliver.
But, bless you, he wasn't there. He was not anywhere,
the Nottingham people said. And some went so far as
to say there was no Mr. Sympson.

Who then?

Who was Gulliver?

There can't be travels unless there's a traveller, —
that's certain. If Mr. Gulliver didn't bring away those
small cattle in his pocket from Blefuscu, — which Capt.
Biddel saw, and Capt. Biddel's mate saw, — where did
he bring them from? or if Mr. Gulliver didn't fetch them
himself, who did?

Everybody asked, and for a good while nobody knew.
At last it all came out. There was no Gulliver, and
there was no Sympson, — only Dean Swift, a queer sort
of Irish clergyman, who saw in his own library every
thing that Gulliver professed to have seen. And this
Dean Swift was as strange a creature as any that Mr.
Gulliver saw.

He was a child of English parents, though he was
born in Ireland, and lived most of his life in Ireland.

Sir William Temple had married a relative of Swift's
mother, and therefore he was befriended by Sir William

Temple, and through him came to know a great many
distinguished people of England, — the King among the
rest. He had a university education, and a powerful
and acute mind, and enormous ambition. These things
would have made him a distinguished man, even if he
had never known Sir William Temple and never known
the King.

But he was an utterly selfish man; and though he was
admired by thousands, he was loved by very few.

That queer story of Gulliver, I have told you of, was
written by him, — not so much to amuse his readers as
to ridicule the people he had met about the court of
England. He loved dearly to ridicule people whom he
disliked; and I think he disliked nearly the whole human
race.

He wanted to be a Bishop; but Archbishop Sharp
told the Queen that he was unfit to be a Bishop; and I
think Sharp was right. A man who is doing his best
only when he is saying (or writing) harsh, witty things of
other people, is not the man for Bishop, or clergyman
either.

And yet — so strange a creature was this Dean Swift
— he did, at one time, make himself respected and held
in good esteem as a parish priest. Not such a man, we
may be sure, as the excellent Dr. Primrose; but he filled
up the measure of his duties with a sturdy zeal, and for
the poor or those who were beneath him in position, he
never had bitter words. He gave in charity too, but
often with such look of scorn as made it hard to accept
his gifts. At the last, too, — to do him justice, — he left
a large sum to endow a hospital for lunatics; and if he
could have had his way, and had possessed money

enough, I think he would have clapped half the world
into such an asylum.   A very great man, to be sure —
as his writings and his influence show; but a soured
man ; with good instincts sometimes struggling up to
light; and sometimes amazing people by sudden explo-
sions of generosity; but yet — all through his life, making ten men hate and fear him, where he made one love
him.

It must be said that his boyhood was a hard one: he
had no father to direct or win him; he was poor; he
only gained his education by the charity of an uncle
whom he never loved, and of whom, in his savage way,
he always spoke scornfully ; he quarrelled with his
teachers.   His only sister married badly, and he never
forgave her for it ; and, though he came afterward to
give support to her family, he did it grudgingly.   He
quarrelled with Sir William Temple, who was one of the
gentlest and most amiable of men ; and when he came,
by his splendid talents, to be associated with the first
men in England, — there were few of them in political
life with whom he did not sooner or later find himself at
war.

He lived when Pope lived, and Gay and Bolingbroke
and Steele and Defoe, the author of "Robinson Crusoe."
But I think he never knew this last, and I dare say
thought of him as a tile-maker and a quack.   Yet there
can be no doubt that he read " Robinson Crusoe," which
was published only five or six years before Gulliver's
travels ; and the minute careful descriptions in this last
remind one very much of the pains-taking descriptions
in the voyages of Crusoe.

Dean Swift's Love.

Of domestic comforts Swift knew very little, and perhaps cared little. In his early life he had met Esther Johnson, a charming young person, who was living under the guardianship of Sir William Temple. Under his

Dean Swift.

direction he became her tutor; he admired her quickness; perhaps he admired her beauty: certain it is that he so won upon her that she gave her heart and faith to him wholly. She was that " Stella " whom all the world came to know through his poems.

When he went to take a parish in Ireland, she followed with an elderly lady friend, and took a cottage near to his parsonage. There she lived for years — people wondering at this strange friendship; she, poor girl, believing her idol, the great Dean, could do nothing wrong. In later life he did indeed marry her privately, but she never came to make glad any home of his ; nor would he — though she entreated it again and again — ever publicly acknowledge the marriage. Beside her death-bed he did relent; but poor Esther Johnson said it was too late ; and she died with a blighted name, and heart-broken.

This was bad enough : but more remains to be told. At the very time when "Stella" was receiving fond letters from this strange Dean — when he never went to England without declaring to her how hard it was to be away — when he was writing fierce political pamphlets, and pushing intrigues at Court ; he was writing letters — quite as fond as those to " Stella " — to a wealthy and beautiful Miss Van-homrig, who is known as the "Vanessa" of some of his best verses. She was highly educated ; she admired the Dean ; they read together : their intimacy was such that all who knew of it believed that he wished and intended to make her his wife. She was led to believe this too : she never doubted Dr. Swift — not even when rumors came to her ear of the true story of "Stella." But, finding out with her woman's wit the real name of "Stella," she wrote to her a letter, asking what claim she had to the protection and love of Dean Swift.

It was after the private marriage; and "Stella" told all, and sent "Vanessa's" letter to the Dean. Fast as horses would carry him the Dean rode away to that beautiful home of Miss Van-homrig, where he had met such kindly greetings — where over and over they two had read poetry together under the shade of the laurel boughs, — laurels of "Vanessa's" own planting, and all planted in honor of the Dean — he did not now slacken pace until he was at the door; he passed into the room where the poor, shrinking, frightened Vanessa waited her fate. He threw her letter wide open upon the table, and with an oath of defiance turned upon his heel, and strode out of the house, — never to enter it again.

She, poor woman, whose heart had gone out to his, bowed underneath this blast of his fury. Three weeks after this, they buried her — the victim of Dean Swift's rage and double dealing.

Do you think this was the sort of a man to make a clergyman of? And yet he could so impose on men of eminence, that the great Addison wrote on the fly-leaf of a little book which he gave him, — "To Dr. Jonathan Swift; the most agreeable companion, the truest friend, and the greatest genius of his age."

Certainly he was a rare genius. No other English writer has ever put words together in a way which shows more surely and more sharply his real meaning; and none ever put more meaning into his words. If he were only less coarse and less indecent, — for he is often both, — no better model for strong, clear writing could be given you. As it is, I would advise only the reading of the Liliput voyage of Gulliver.

And what old age do you think befell this great man? No calm, — no peace in it; no quietude of home; no children ever, fondled him. He grew so petulant and irritable, that no one wanted to live in the same house with him. Then came moodiness and melancholy. For a year he said never a word to any one. At last that great mind of his — which was joined to no heart at all — broke down, and went out. Yet still he lingered; he ate; he slept; he paced his chamber — knowing nothing — saying nothing that was worth saying; and only hired keepers were with him at his death.

If he were alive to-day, and at his best, we might like to have him make our dictionaries for us, or go to Washington for us; but of a certainty — knowing him as we do — we should never want him to preach Christianity for us, or to sit down with us at our firesides.

A Brobdingnag Book.

VI.

AN IRISH STORY-TELLER.

Who was She?

DID you ever hear of Gretna-Green, and of Gretna-Green marriages?

Gretna is a small place in Scotland, only a little way over the English border, as you go from Carlisle to Dumfries; and it used to be famous as a place for run-away couples to go and be married — a thing that it was much easier to do, without consent of relatives, under the Scotch law, than under the English law.

Well, in the year 1763 — the year when poor Goldsmith was getting into trouble with his landlady, and had the "Vicar of Wakefield" still in his drawer — there drove up to the inn at Gretna a fine carriage with a young gentleman in it, hardly nineteen years old, who was an Oxford student; and he brought with him a young girl only seventeen; and these runaways were married there by the blacksmith of the village, who was also justice of the peace.

I suppose the parents were indignant; but I think

they forgave them afterward. The young wife lived
only a few years ; but she left to her husband two
children. The oldest, a boy, was brought up in a very
strange way, — yet a way which had been commended
by a French philosopher, — Rousseau (who never had a
child that he cared for). This young Oxford man was
at this time a great admirer of Rousseau : so his boy
did what he chose to do, and nothing that he did not
choose. He was never punished ; wore no clothing
beyond what decency required ; and grew up, as anybody might expect, a strong, active, ungovernable, bare-
armed and bare-legged young savage. He took a strong
liking for the sea, just when his father would have been
glad to keep him on land ; and to sea he went ; and at
sea he kept — until in after days he went to America,
married there, and settled near to Georgetown in South
Carolina, where, it is said, some of his descendants still
live.

The second child of this runaway match was a
daughter, who grew up to be one of the best-known
women in all Europe ; and her name — if you have not
guessed it already — was Maria Edgeworth.

Her father — Richard Lovell Edgeworth, married
again ; in fact, he married a third and a fourth wife
before he was sixty ; and he had a great company of
children, who lived with him in a huge country house
near to Longford in the centre of Ireland. Here Maria
Edgeworth went, when she was only four years old ; here
she grew into such love for Ireland and the Irish, that
she called herself an Irishwoman, and was proud to be
so called ; and here she wrote those stories which were
the delight of all young people forty years ago, and

those novels which were the delight of all the grown
people of her time. — You never heard of them? Well,
well! Yet it is not so very long ago that she was alive
there, — a good, kindly old lady ; and her stepmother
— the latest wife of Richard Edgeworth — died only the
other day (1864).

It is quite too soon to forget good Miss Edgeworth
and her books. Why, in my school-days, the fellow who
had not read " Eton Montem," and " Forrester," and
" Waste not, Want not," was not counted much of a
reader. There were long words in them, and some
prosiness, maybe (Dr. Johnson, who set the example
of long words, was the great man in her young days, you
must remember) ; but there was a good plot in her
stories, and a good winding-up. You couldn't tell now,
if you were to read one of her books, what church she
attended, or what party she voted with ; but you could
find, scattered up and down, such talk as would show —
that honesty and common sense and good manners and
good morals and all charities were always venerated by
her, and always taught by her.

Her Stories.

I don't think I shall forget to the last day of my life,
the long white Chalk-Hill near to Dunstable, where
Paul and his little sister "scotched" the wheels of the
chaises that went toiling up, so that the horses might
take a breathing-spell. The story was in the " Parents'
Assistant ;" and there was a quaint old cut showing
Paul with his " scotcher," and sister Anne, and the old
grandmother — talking over the guinea which had been
given the children by accident.

Would he keep it?—would he return it?   Of course we knew how it would be; and the sturdy honesty and

Basket-Woman.

pluck of the lad as he went bustling through the inn-yard at Dunstable was more refreshing than the eighth commandment repeated ten times over.

Some of us made "scotchers," to look like Paul's, out of blocks and broom-handles; but there were no chaise-wheels and no long chalk-hills to help us out; and no guineas dropped into *our* hats by accident or otherwise. If there had been, I think we should have caught — all the same — the infection of good Miss Edgeworth's straightforward honesty. Healthy, cheery, unhesitating honesty is always catching.

The fact is, that homely old truths, which nobody in his senses ever thought of disputing, lie at the bottom of most of Miss Edgeworth's pleasant stories, and put their color on them from beginning to end.

She doesn't take the sly way of covering up a moral pill in a spoonful of jelly — so that a boy shall bolt it without knowing it ; nor does she tie the lesson she wants to teach upon the end of her stories — like a snapper ; but it runs all through them, and is so strong and sound and good that every boy's common sense makes him stand up stoutly for her little heroes.

Take that old tale of "Waste not, Want not." Mr. Meacham is a shrewd, practical, kindly-disposed man, who — having no sons of his own — has taken a couple of nephews to bring up and care for.

Hal is free and easy ; and has been brought up to have a great respect for people with a great trail — whether of titles or of silk. How the boy does worship Lady Diana Sweepstakes and her sons !

Ben, the other nephew, is thoughtful, quiet, careful, plodding, and doesn't think of running after boys because they are Lady Diana's sons.

Mr. Meacham — wanting to test the working ways of his two nephews — gives to each a big parcel to undo. Hal goes daintily about his task, — puzzles over the knots, — gets petulant, — whips out his knife, and cuts all clean. Ben sets himself sturdily to a careful untying of the fastenings, and saves a good bit of whipcord. Next day Mr. Meacham gives each of them a top — but without strings. Ben, by his steady care of yesterday, is provided with a capital one. Hal — in a gust of perplexity — at last pulls off his hat-band, and uses it up.

Presently afterward, a great archery match is to come off under the patronage of Lady Diana. Both are provided with bows and arrows, — thanks to uncle Meacham : and both, by a little practice, come to be good shots. Hal wants a white and green uniform to wear — since Lady Diana's boys are to have such. Ben does not care so much to do things because Lady Di's boys do them ; and puts his money into a good winter coat, that will be of service when the archery day is gone by.

Well, the time for the match comes at length. Hal is very fine in his green and white ; but it is something cold and windy ; and his hat — for want of that band which went to top-spinning some days before — goes spinning over a ploughed field, where Hal must needs follow, and comes back with his green and white uniform woefully draggled and besmeared with red mud. He could bear this better if he did not catch a sneering look from Lady Diana and Lady Diana's boys : those who worship fashion must take fashion's sneers. However, he stands up bravely to the shooting. The Sweepstakes boys have made good ventures ; Hal does fairly at the first two shots (they have three each) ; but at the third — twang ! goes his bow-string, — hopelessly broken.

Ben shoots as well ; is mighty comfortable, too, in his snug linsey-woolsey coat ; but it could not bar him

against accident. His bow-string gives out at the second shot. Ben is not flustered one jot : he pulls out
that bit of whipcord which he had saved from his par-
cel-fastening, and which had done service with his top,
— adjusts it to his bow, — takes new aim, and with two
capital shots — one after the other — wins the match.

I suspect that little experience — as recorded in the
" Parents' Assistant " — has led to the saving of a great
deal of whipcord first and last : and I suspect it has
lessened the eagerness with which some boys — even
American boys — will go hunting after familiarity with
the showy Lady Dianas and the Lady Diana's sons.
Miss Edgeworth did not believe in fustian.

Then there was that jolly story — as we easily thought
it — of the " Limerick Gloves." What a pig-headed
British obstinacy in the old verger Jonathan Hill, with
his — " What I say, I say ; and what I think, I think."
We had seen such people, though they did not wear
wigs like the verger of Hereford. There was the stout
wife too, who set him upon the hunt for unreal troubles,
and carried her head so high ; and the pretty Phœbe,
with the bang in her hair, looking demure, but very
constant in thinking well of Mr. Brian O'Neill, whatever
papa might do or say.

It looked as if there were a great Popish plot to come
out in the story, and as if the Hereford Cathedral were
to be blown up ; but it ends in a scare about a mere rat-
hole under the church wall, and in the pretty Phœbe
wearing her Limerick gloves ; and " no perfume ever
was so delightful to her lover " (who was Brian O'Neill)
" as the smell of the rose-leaves in which they had been
kept." The moral of the tale is, — we have no right

to suspect people of roguery and arson because they do not sing out of our hymn-book.

I have no doubt Phœbe and O'Neill married ; but Miss Edgeworth doesn't say so. In fact, few of her stories are love-stories in the ordinary sense. She never married herself ; and I dare say saw no reason why a story — like a life — might not be a good one without being rounded off with a marriage.

Limerick Gloves.

Nearly all of her stories were written in that old country-house in Ireland. There was almost always a troop of children in it, as I have said, whom she loved, and who loved her. The father, too, was a companion and a helper in all her work ; for he had bravely given over all the wild courses of his younger days, and was one of the best of landlords ; seeking always for means to help on his work-people, and so knitting their interests with his own, that in the rebellion of 1798, when so many brave young Irishmen went to the scaffold, and

so many homes were desolated, the Edgeworth house
(though they were obliged to leave it for a time, in the
madness of the outbreak) was wholly unharmed. Even
the pens and papers upon Miss Edgeworth's table were
found, at their return, precisely as she had left them.

Edgeworth.

An avenue of gaunt old trees leads up to the mansion
from the high road ; and the library windows look out
upon lawn and garden, which were always in the old
time carefully kept. And it is a wonderful thing, and
worth the telling — that this good lady authoress never
had her " moods " — never neglected commonest every-
day duties, and actually did her book-making work sur-
rounded by the family, — with only such retirement as
she could gain by placing her quaint little writing-table
(still preserved) in a corner of the great library, which
was also the common sitting-room.

But it was an orderly and a cheery household. **Mr.**
Edgeworth writes to Dr. Darwin in 1796 — "I do not
think one tear a month is shed in this house, nor the
voice of reproof heard." The son who had been bred
half a savage was gone at this time ; else I think he
would have amused himself with pinching the fat arms
of the little ones.

I cannot show you a portrait of Miss Edgeworth ; for
she would never consent to sit for one. She was not
beautiful, but very comely, and had those virtues which
almost compensate for beauty — extremest cleanliness
and neatness of dress and person.

Forester.

Upon the whole, I think the best short story of Miss
Edgeworth's is that which she calls " Forester ; " it is
certainly worth every boy's reading. I can only give
you a sketch of it.

The hero was the son of a strange English gentleman, who had very curious notions about society and
education, — not very unlike those which Mr. Edgeworth held when he was making a half-savage of his
oldest son.

Forester's father died when the lad was nineteen ;
and he was placed under the guardianship of Dr. Campbell, a clever and learned man, who had a clever son
Henry, and a pretty lass of a daughter called Flora.

Forester was brave and generous and truthful ; but
he had been taught to believe that cleanliness and good
manners and the usual forms of cultivated society were
idle things, not worthy of the consideration of a reflect-

ing man ; and he brought his half-savage habits into the family of the good Dr. Campbell. The Campbells, seeing his better qualities, bore with him patiently ; but there was a certain Lady Mackenzie, with her son Archibald, living under the same roof — very pretentious and artificial and shallow, both of them. These lose no occasion to ridicule the shortcomings of poor Forester, who finds that the ridicule of the shallow, if well informed in the ways of the world, is very irritating. He pays back ridicule with a noisy contempt ; and his sense of truth is not kept in check by any regard for the feelings of others. He would have lived as independent as Robinson Crusoe, if he could, and with as little practice of the ordinary courtesies of society. He had been taught to think that a polished manner must needs go always with a selfish indolence ; and he showed his hate for it by wanton disregard of proprieties, and by choosing his companions among those beneath him, whom he honored only because they were without any fashionable gloss.

I suppose that most of big-brained boys go through this state of feeling at some period of their youth ; but they never get on very well in life until they master it and hold it decently in check.

Forester's wrong-headedness puts him in the way of incurring a good many damaging suspicions — that are slyly fed by the Mackenzies, who hate the lad's coarseness, and are jealous of his cleverness. But this he could bear bravely enough, — with the knowledge that he was honest and true. But when his slovenliness and disregard for appearances exposed him to the open ridicule of a company of well-bred people — as it did upon a memorable evening at his friends, the Campbells, he forswears all further intercourse with such people — packs up his wardrobe, — writes an adieu to the Campbells, and goes to live with an industrious, simple-minded gardener.

He finds, however, that the gardener and the gardener's people — however simple-minded they may be — are just as self-seeking as those he has left ; and that it

"Forester."

is none the better for being coarsely shown. He learns how to plant flowers, and enjoys it ; but he doesn't find any delightful Arcadia with the gardener.

He conceals his name so that old acquaintances shall know nothing of him ; yet his new acquaintances are not satisfying : so he changes quarters, and establishes himself in the office of a great brewery. Oddly enough, he doesn't find the clerks and apprentices here altogether perfect. He gets his dismission at an early day, because he will not join his fellow clerks in supporting some false report to the officers of excise.

He next undertakes employment with a bookseller and printer, whom he has encountered accidentally, and with whom he doubtless hopes to find purity without any pretence or parade. I doubt if he did ; so does Miss Edgeworth.

Meantime he had been practising extravagant charities — siding with poor street people in quarrels he knew nothing of — thrusting himself into situations by his independent bravado, that made him easily suspected of bad deeds. Indeed, it came to that pass at last, that he was fairly arrested as party to a theft of which he knew no more than the man in the moon.

As an independent young citizen who wanted to live his own life without thanks to anybody — there was no one to help him. But as young Forester — when his name came to be known — and former companion to young Henry Campbell, the old Doctor and all his friends came forward to aid him in spite of himself. These establish very clearly the honesty of the young man ; but in making this clear, it was equally well proven that he had acted with very great folly. Perhaps it was some consolation to him to know that the real culprit — so far as there was any culprit at all in the matter of the theft — was his old enemy, the elegant Archibald Mackenzie.

Forester is brought to think better of the Campbells — gentlemanly as they are ; and he is taught, too, to pay more regard than had been his habit to those formalities of society, which the usage and good-fellowship of the world — for a few centuries past — have laid down for law. He gave over the hope of fighting windmills and carrying off honor ; or of overleaping the customs of civilized life at a bound. In the excess of his new-found tolerance, it is stated that he condescends to

take a few dancing-lessons.   He goes back to his old
intimacy with the Campbells — father and son and
daughter.   He wears clean linen — does not put on
Crusoe goat-skins; thinks no worse of people for saying "Good-morning" cheerily and to all the world ; does
not consider a shabby coat or a coarse speech of neces-
sity a reason for showing favor ; and the curtain of the
little story drops upon our hero — dancing a Scotch reel
with the pretty Flora Campbell!

Whether they made a match of it, Miss Edgeworth
does not say, and has no need to say.   The tale is
pointed with a moral, though it be not blazoned with a
marriage.

VII.

TWO FRENCH FRIENDS.

Burst of Revolution.

I REMEMBER that in my old Geography — a little square, fat book, most unlike the Geographies which I observe spread out under the eyes and elbows of youngsters nowadays — the Frenchman was pictured and described as an extremely limber and graceful gentleman, taking off his hat with a wide flourish to ladies in great furbelows, or else dancing with others of like elegance around a tall tree ; and I always found it very hard to believe how so gay and polite and festive gentlemen should have taken it into their hearts or heads to engage in the bloody work of those " Days of Terror," which were also spoken of in the Geography. I have discovered since, that dancing men and women are often very cruel, and do not care on whose toes they tread.

You have all heard, I dare say, of the French Revolution. But do you know how it came about, and what its terrors were ?

It came about because there had been a great many wicked kings and wicked nobles in France, who had lived only for their own selfish ends, and had considered the people as beasts of burden, to be used to help them forward in their pleasure-seeking and their money-getting. If they wanted war for any ambitious purpose of their own, whole regions were desolated, and sons and fathers and husbands swept away down the bloody path that war always makes. If they wanted service of any kind, — whether honest labor or vile labor, — children were torn from parents, and new-married wives from their husbands.

But the poorest of the French people were so ignorant, and had lived in a state of slavish dread of those who were above them in rank, for so long a time, that perhaps they would have borne their trials longer — if it had not happened that very many among the richer people, and the better educated ones suffered too, by reason of quarrels with the nobles, or quarrels among themselves, or abuses of the king or his courtiers. Among the most fearful of these abuses were those which were committed under the authority of what were called *lettres du cachet*, or letters with the royal seal. Throughout the reigns of Louis XIV. and of Louis XV., this sort of tyranny was common. Thus, if a noble bore a grudge against some neighbor, and wished to take him out of the way, he would apply to the king or to a royal minister, and beg or buy an order with the royal seal upon it : — Under authority of this royal order, he would send a file of soldiers to seize his enemy, and thrust him into a prison of the state, where he might spend years without communication with wife or friends.

Friends or family would not know, indeed, whither he had gone ; and so secretly would the work be done, that they could not tell when or by whom he was torn away. Sometimes an old, white-haired man, who had been almost forgotten, would suddenly appear among his acquaintances again, after twenty years of dungeon life.

If you should ever read Mr. Dickens's "Tale of Two Cities," — and it is one of the strongest stories he wrote, and well worth your reading, — you will find a thrilling narrative of the imprisonment of a French physician, — who was torn away from his young wife, and for sixteen long years never heard if she were alive or dead. No wonder that his mind gave way, and that when he found liberty at last, he was a poor decrepit shadow of a man.

There is also another terrible story of abuse under these *lettres du cachet*, which is said to be wholly true, and which appeared in a book called "Letters from France," by Helen Maria Williams, — an English lady who passed much time in France before the Revolution, and who was herself a prisoner in the Temple, under the rule of Robespierre. Her story was about a black-hearted father, who, — under cover of one of these kingly orders or letters, — caused his own son, who had offended him, to be snatched away from his family, and to be buried in a dungeon for years. In fact, there was hardly any crime against persons that might not be permitted under shelter of one of those terrible "letters" of the king.

What would you think, pray, if our President, or Gen. Sherman, might issue a letter with the State seal

affixed, which would empower any marshal or politician —
or whoever might gain possession of the letter — to seize
upon any enemy of his at dead of night, and bear him
off to prison, and keep him there so long as he might
choose? Would not such a power, unchecked by any
courts of justice or by law, make of our country — or of
any country — a very doleful place to live in?

And can you wonder that those poor people in that
far-away France, and in that far-away time (nearly a
hundred years now), should have chafed under it, and
talked bitterly and threateningly; until after a while
their angry and threatening talk grew into a great tempest that swept through the Paris streets like a whirl-
wind?

No wonder they were maddened; no wonder their
passion got the better of their judgment; no wonder
the population, led on by enraged men, worked deeds
of cruelty which made all Europe shudder. Very great
wrongs, however orderly, are almost always balanced —
sooner or later — by very great and disorderly avenge-
ment.

When that tempest of madness I was speaking of just
now first swept through the streets of Paris, in the reign
of Louis XVI., it drove the crazed people in herds, to
glut their vengeance upon those who were keeping captives in chains, within the great prison of the Bastille.
This was a grim and dismal-looking building upon the
borders of Paris, with sluggish water around it; and
its door was entered by a draw-bridge. Toward the
frowning walls of this prison (there is only a tall bronze
column upon the spot now) the populace of the city
rushed headlong, with whatever weapons they could lay

hands upon. Butchers took their cleavers, stable-men their forks, carters their heavy oaken stakes, carpenters their axes; and there were thousands with guns and cutlasses, while brawny women carried huge pistols.

The Bastille.

The soldiers who guarded the prison were so frightened by the sights and sounds of this tempest of the people's fury, that they could hardly make any opposing fight at all. The governor of the prison, seeing what mad rage he must encounter, would have blown up the huge building altogether; and had actually laid the match to do so, but the soldiers rebelled, and forced him to surrender. Then the raging mob flowed in; and those who wore the uniform of the king were smitten to death. The dungeon gates were unlocked, and prisoners staggered out, who had not seen the sun for dozens and scores of years.

Days of Terror.

A beautiful girl was caught sight of, flying down one of the great stairways. She was straightway seized upon by those who believed her to be a daughter of the governor, and would have been burned in the court-yard had not a few generous soldiers stolen her away, and secreted her until the sack was over. As for the governor, — who was a marquis and the king's friend, — they cut off his head, and bore it bleeding from the top of a pike-staff, all down the street; and all down the street poured the mad, rejoicing rabble, slaying many another as they went, and carrying the trophies with them, — gory heads on pikes, or gory heads on chafing-dishes carried by women.

As it was on that day, so it was on many a day thereafter, and for many a week and month; and for years, whoever was a noble, or friend of the hated nobles, — or rich, or friend of the hated rich, — lived, if he lived at all in that city of revolution, in great dread and danger.

There was not much feeling at the first against Louis XVI., for he was a far better king than those who had gone before him. He was kindly at heart, and what we might call nowadays a gentlemanly, amiable man, — with not much force of character, and disposed to yield to the opinions of those who had been his old advisers. These, by their obstinacy, brought him very soon to grief. The people forced him to trial, and there was a forced condemnation. His head, too, fell before the fury of the enraged people, and was held up by the executioner upon the scaffold, for the thronging mob to look upon.

This poor king had left behind him in the prison a son, whom he had taught, as he best could in those dreary prison hours, arithmetic and geography. Do you think the boy ever forgot those lessons, or ever forgot the sorrow, and the loud wailings of his mother — the queen, when the king went out to his death?

A little after this, those crazy ones who were governing France gave over this prince boy to the care of a shoemaker and his wife, — to whom they furnished a lodgement in the prison; and they did this in order, as they said, that the bringing-up of the boy might be as low as that of the lowest of the people. Poor boy! poor prince!

A little later, Marie Antoinette, the queen, was taken out of her dungeon to go to trial: they called it a trial, for the sake of decency; but I think they knew how it would end, before they called on her to appear. If the judges before whom she stood had said she was innocent and must go free, I am sure that the wives of the wine-sellers, and the fish-women, and the hags of Paris, would have snatched her away, and carried her off to execution, — if they had not slain her with their own bread-knives in the street.

These mad people had such a thirst for blood!

It was better perhaps that the judges should say the queen must be beheaded, as they did, than that these wild women should cut her in pieces.

She certainly died an easier death by the guillotine.

Another famous woman who fell under the hands of the executioner in these bloody days, and whom we do not know whether most to pity or to admire, was Charlotte Corday.

She was of humble family, in Normandy. No one in Paris had ever heard of her when she left her home in

early July, 1793, to come up to the bloody city. Yet what she did, and what happened to her within one week, have made her name known everywhere.

She had a lover who was suspected by the revolutionary tribunal, and who was assassinated by order of Marat, — who was the most cruel and the most hated of all the men who governed.

Charlotte Corday.

Charlotte Corday determined to avenge her lover, and free France of the monster Marat. So she journeyed up to Paris, — went to the home of Marat, — found some excuse for admission, — engaged him in talk (for she was winning in manner, and intelligent), and, seizing her chance, plunged a dagger in his bosom.

There were many in Paris who gave a sigh of relief when they heard of this murder; but there were howling thousands who clamored for the blood of poor Charlotte Corday. A young man offered to die in her place; but this could not be. There was a sharp, quick trial, and within a week, — in her little Norman sacque, — and in her Norman cap, she too went through the streets to take her turn under the sharp, swift knife of the guillotine.

The Guillotine.

You don't know what the guillotine is ?

I will tell you. Perhaps you have sometimes seen the great knives sliding up and down in a frame, by which hay and straw are cut for horses. Well, imagine, if you can, a knife like those, — only a great deal larger and a great deal sharper, - -working up and down in grooves like the straw-cutter. Then imagine such a knife at the top of two grooved posts some eight feet high, with a great weight resting on it ; then fancy the poor victim lying at the foot of these posts, with the bared neck placed directly between the grooves ; next imagine the headsman, — as he was called, — pulling a cord which sets the great knife free — to come — clanging down with an awful thud ———

It does dreadfully quick work : but, for all that, it is the most humane way of executing capital punishment : — if there be any humanity in it at all — which I doubt.

The machine was called *guillotine*, after a Dr. Guillotin, who, in the French Assembly in 1791, proposed a better way of cutting off people's heads than the old way of doing it by an axe ; which he said was a clumsy way, and clumsy headsmen sometimes made bad work of it. But Dr. Guillotin was not the inventor, as some books will tell you ; nor did he lose his own head by it, as other books will tell you.

In 1792 the question of finding some new way of
execution was referred to Dr. Antoine Louis, the Secre-
tary of the College of Surgeons ; and he advised such a
method as had been hinted at by Dr. Guillotin the year
before. They had therefore a machine made for trial
by one Schmidt, who was a knife-maker. Finding it
worked well, after trial, they adopted it ; and people
called it at first "Louisette." But Dr. Louis said he
didn't invent it, or make it. (Webster's Unabridged
Dictionary, which is so rarely wrong, makes a mistake
in saying he did invent it.)

So the people went back on the name of Dr. Guillotin — all because a poet of that day had made some
jingling rhymes, in which the honor had been referred
to him.

The real truth is, that a machine like it had been used
in Italy, at Genoa, two hundred years before ; and in
England, at Halifax ; and in Scotland, at Edinburgh,
more than a hundred years before. The Scotch people
had called it " The Maiden."

It is a dreadful machine, and does very quick work,
as I know ; for I have myself seen a man's head taken
off by it ; and I never wish to see such a sight again.

And now, why do you suppose I have run over this
dismal bit of history ? Only as a sort of introduction
to two of your good friends, — a man and a woman who
lived in Paris through all this time of blood, and who
yet have written the two most charming and pleasant
stories for children that are anywhere to be found in
the French language.

Paul and Virginia.

The name of the first story is "Paul and Virginia;" and the name of its author, Bernardin de St. Pierre. He was born at Havre, a seaport town at the mouth of the Seine, and went to school there until he was twelve; but while he was at school he fell in with a translation of "Robinson Crusoe," and he loved the book so much that he came to love adventure more than books, and begged for permission to go over seas with an uncle, who was bound for Martinique.

And he went there, and saw first in that island (which you will find on your atlas among the West Indies) the bananas, and palms, and orange-trees, and all that rich tropical growth, which afterward he scattered up and down upon the pages of his story of "Paul and Virginia."

But the boy Bernardin did not stay in Martinique: he grew homesick, and went back to France, and studied engineering in Paris; and before he was twenty had gone away again to Malta, which is a strongly fortified little island in the Mediterranean, lying southward of Italy. He did not stay, however, in Malta; for he fought a duel there, which made it an unsafe place for him.

Not long after this he obtained a position under the famous Empress Catherine of Russia, and had strange adventures in Poland; where it is said a beautiful Polish princess would have married the young French engineer, but her friends took good care she should not commit what was counted so great an indiscretion.

He then went to his old home at Havre again; but his family was scattered, and the home broken. He next gained an appointment as engineer to the Isle of France,—which was another tropical island near to Madagascar, in the Indian Ocean. After five or six

Bernardin de St. Pierre.

years here, among the bananas and the palm-trees, he went back to Paris—without business, without money, almost without friends. This was his own fault, however; for he was reckless and petulant and proud.

He began now to think of printing books, though he

was past thirty-four. His first venture was a story of
his voyage to the Isle of France; afterward he passed
many years working at what he called " Studies of Nature." He could hardly find a publisher for this. At
last, however, he bargained with M. Didot to print it,
— and Didot was the most celebrated printer in France.
Not only did he print the book of the adventurous Bernardin, but he gave him his daughter for a wife.

I suppose that this author gave a great deal more of
study and of care to his book on Nature, than he did to
the little story of " Paul and Virginia." Yet it was this
last — which was published some two years or more
before the capture of the Bastille — which gave him his
great fame.

Where there was one reader for his other books,
there were twenty readers for " Paul and Virginia."
In those fierce days when the Revolution was ripening,
and a gigantic system of privileges was breaking up
and consuming away, — like straw in fire, — this little
tender, simple story, with its gushes of sentiment, and
its warm, tropical atmosphere, was being thumbed in
porters' lodges, and was read in wine-shops, and hidden
under children's pillows, and was sought after by noble
women, — and women who were not noble, — and by
priests who slipped it into their pockets with their
books of prayer. Even the hard, flinty-faced young
officer of artillery, Napoleon Bonaparte, had read it
with delight, and, in after-years, greeted the author
with the imperial demand, — " When, M. St. Pierre, will
you give us another ' Paul and Virginia ' ? "

It is only a simple tale, tenderly told. A boy and
girl love each other, purely and deeply ; they have grown

up together; they are poor and untaught; but the flowers and fruits are rich around them, and the sweetest odors of the tropics are spent upon the story. Virginia — loving the boy — sails away from their island home to win education in the old world — of France.

Paul and Virginia.

The boy grieves; and studies that he may match in himself the accomplishments which Virginia is gaining in Europe. At last the ship is heralded which speeds her back. In a frenzy of delight Paul sees the great ship sweep down toward the shore.

But clouds threaten; a wild swift storm bursts over the beautiful island; there is gloom and wreck; and a fair, lifeless form is stranded on the sands.

Poor Virginia! Poor Paul!

Then — two graves, with the name of the story over them. And the birds sing, and the tropical flowers bloom as before.

This is all there is of it.

Do you not wonder that so slender a tale could take any hold upon a people who were ingulfed in the terrors of that mad revolution? Why was it?

Partly, I think, because the dainty and tender tone of the story-teller offered such strange contrast to the fierce wrangle of daily talk; partly also, because in the breaking down of all the old society laws and habits of living in France, it was a relief to catch this sweet glimpse of the progress of an innocent life and innocent love — albeit of children — under purely natural influences.

It is worth your reading, were it only that you may see what tender and exaggerated sentiment was relished by this strange people, at a time when they were cutting off heads in the public square, by hundreds.

It is specially worth reading in its French dress, for its choice and simple and limpid language.

The Siberian Wanderer.

We come now to talk of the other book of which I spoke. It is by Madame Cottin, and is called "Elizabeth; or, The Exiles of Siberia."

Siberia, you know, is a country of great wastes, where

snows lie fearfully deep in winter, and winds howl across the bleak, vast levels; and wolves abound. It is under the dominion of Russia; and to this pitiless country the emperor of Russia was wont to send prisoners of state in close exile — where their names were unknown, and all communication would be cut off; and where they would live as if dead.

Well, Elizabeth was the daughter of such a prisoner; who, with his wife, lived in a lonely habitation in the midst of this dreary region. She grows up in this desolate solitude, knowing only those tender parents, and their gnawing grief. She knows nothing of their crime, or exile, or judge, or real name. But as she ripens into girlhood the parents cannot withhold their confidence; and she comes to know of their old, and cherished, and luxurious home on the Polish plains, — which is every day in their memory.

From this time forth the loving daughter has but one controlling thought; and that is, — how she may restore these sorrowful parents to their home, and to the world.

It is a child's purpose; and opposed to it is the purpose of the Autocrat of all the Russias. But then, courage and persistence are noble things, and they win more triumphs than you could believe. They will win them over school lessons, and bad habits, and bad temper, — just as surely as they win them in the battles of the world.

So, upon the desolate plains of Siberia the fair young girl plots — and plots. How could this frail creature set about the undoing of an imperial edict, and the restoration of father and mother to life and happiness once more? Over and over she pondered in the solemn quietude of those wintry Siberian nights, upon all the ways which might avail to gain her purpose. At last came the resolve — and a very bold one it was — to make the journey on foot, from their place of exile to the Russian capital; never doubting — in the fulness of her faith — that if she could once gain a hearing from the emperor, she could win his favor, and put an end to her father's exile.

Ah! what could she know of the depth of state crimes, or of the bitterness of royal hate, or of that weary march of over two thousand miles across all the breadth of Russia?

She had not the courage to tell of this resolution to her parents; but kept it ever uppermost in her thoughts as months and years rolled on, and she gained strength; while the dear lives she most cherished were wasting with grief and toil in the wintry solitudes.

One friend she made her confidant: this was the son of the governor of Tobolsk, who, in his hunting expeditions, had come unawares upon the retired cabin of her father, and thereafter repeated twice or thrice his visit. He was charmed by her beauty and tenderness, and would have spoken of love; but she had no place in her heart for that. Always uppermost in her thought was the weary walk to be accomplished, and the pardon to be sought.

The young hunter could not aid her; for intercourse with the exiled family was forbidden, and he had already been summoned away and ordered to regions unknown.

At last, after years of waiting, — Elizabeth being now eighteen, — an old priest came that way who was jour-

neying to the west.   It seemed her golden opportunity.
She declared now, for the first time, her purpose to
her parents.   They expostulated and reasoned with her.
The long way was a drear one ; monarchs were remorse-
less ; they had grown old in exile, and could bear it to
the end.

But the tender girl was more unshaken and steadfast
than they.   She bade them a tearful adieu, and with
the old priest by her side, turned her steps toward the
Russian capital.   Very toilsome it was, and day followed
day, and week week, with wearisome walking; and before the journey was half done the old priest sickened
and died — she nursing him and closing his eyes for
his last sleep — in a cabin by the way.

But still she had no thought of turning back, but
wearily and painfully pressed on.   Week followed week,
and still long roads lay before her.   It will make your
hearts ache to read the story of her toil, — of her bleeding feet, — of her encounters with rude plunderers, —
her struggles with storm and snow and cliff.   There
were great stretches of silent forest; there were broad
rivers to cross; there were gloomy ravines to pass
through ; and her strength was failing, and she had been
robbed of her money, and the winter was coming on ;
and there was no messenger or mail to tell her of the
dear ones she had left in the little cabin of the exile.
But through all, her courage never once failed ; and at
last it rejoiced her heart — to see in the blazing sun-
light, on the edge of the Muscovite plains, the great
shining domes of the palace of Moscow.

Here she was a stranger in a great city ; and the
wilderness of the streets was full of more terrors and

more dangers for her than the wilderness of the vast forests she had crossed in safety. Her very frailty, however, with her earnestness and her appealing look, won upon passers-by; and well-wishers befriended her, and heard her story with amazement. And her story spread, and made other well-wishers aid, until at last she came to the feet of the emperor.

The Wanderer.

They knew — all of them — the tale she had to tell; and the eyes of all pleaded with her so strongly, that her request was granted, and the father set free.

Of course the story glides on very pleasantly after this. She has a government coach to carry her back over that long stretch of foot-travel; she finds her parents yet alive; she somehow has encountered again that stray son of the governor of Tobolsk; and I believe they were married, and all lived happily ever after.

It is not much of a love story however, — except of parental love, — which, after all, is one of the purest kinds of love.

Madame Cottin, who wrote the story, lived, as I said, in the days of the French Revolution, and was married in the year 1790, when she was only seventeen years old. Her husband was very much older, and a rich banker. I doubt if she loved him greatly; there are some things in other books of hers (for she published a great many) which make me think so very strongly. Still I believe she was an honest woman, and struggled to do her duty. I do not think Madame Cottin's other works are to be commended, or that any one reads them very much nowadays. "Elizabeth" — the book of which I have given you the story — was printed in the time of the First Napoleon (1806), and had an immense success. There is hardly a language of Europe in which it is not to be found printed now.

It is a good story. What devotion! — so rare — so true — so tender!

Read it for this, if nothing else; and cherish the memory ever in your young hearts.

It is as good a sermon on the fifth commandment as you will ever hear; and remember — that it was preached by a Frenchwoman, who lived in Paris through the reign of blood.

VIII.

FAIRY REALM.

The Grimm Brothers.

NOT Giant Grim who lives in the "Pilgrim's Progress." Oh, no! it is not that sort of person at all,
about whom I am to tell you, — but of two brothers, who
were born in Germany, — one at Hanau and the other
at Cassel, — only a little time before the outbreak of
that French Revolution of which I have told you
within the last few pages.

There were, indeed, five brothers Grimm of this family; but we have concern now only with two, — Jacob
and William, — who lived much together, and worked
together with a tender friendliness that is rare, even
between brothers. Their youth was full of hardships.
The father died so early that they had only boyish
remembrances of him ; and the good mother — of whom
Jacob speaks most tenderly — was left with so small a
property, that she could with difficulty give them the
commonest schooling. But pluck and industry, with
occasional aid from a good aunt, helped them through.

You must have heard of Cassel; or, if you have ever been in Germany, the chances are that you have seen it, and the palace and gardens of Wilhelmshöhe.

You will remember, perhaps, that Louis Napoleon was sent here after the victory of Sedan. There could hardly have been a more delightful prison — where he had the liberty of the grounds, and a great throng of servants at his command. Every traveller delights in wandering under the embowered walks of the palace grounds. There are trees and flowers of all climates there; there are statues and grottoes; there is a fountain which, when in full blast, throws its water a hundred and ninety feet into the air — being the highest fountain in the world. Then there is a vast flight of stone steps, over which the water sometimes comes bounding down in torrents; and these steps lead up to the colossal Hercules, whose figure crowns the hill, and looks all abroad upon gardens, and mountains, and town. But even better worth seeing than this, or than the museums stocked with rare and curious things, is the view of the lovely valley, which you get from the public square of Cassel.

In the middle of this square stands the statue of the Elector Frederic II. Yet he was not a man who deserved a statue. He indeed brought together the beautiful objects in the museum, and adorned the town by lavish expenditure. This would have been very well, if the moneys had come to him fairly. But how do you suppose he won his vast wealth, — of which the traces are around one everywhere at Cassel? Only by selling the lives of his people.

You will remember, that in any story of the Ameri-

can Revolution which you may have read, there is frequent mention of the "Hessians" who fought for
George of England.

Well, these "Hessians," or hired soldiers, were the
subjects of the Elector Frederic II., of Hesse-Cassel, in
Germany. They were snatched from their homes and
families, — more than twenty-two thousand of them,
between the years 1776 and 1784, — and compelled to
fight over seas, the Elector receiving for their hire
more than twelve millions of dollars; and this was a
sum in that day which would be equal to twenty millions now.

If the brothers Grimm had been of good age in the
time of the Elector Frederic, they might have died,
very likely, on the battle-fields of New Jersey.

But why have I gone over seas to the shadows of
Wilhelmshöhe to find these Grimm brothers? Did
they ever invent good stories? No. Jacob, indeed,
told the story of his life; but there is no invention in
it, — no fairies in it. He says, —

"My father was too early taken from us; and I still
see in spirit the black coffin, the bearers with the yel-
low lemons and the rosemary in their hands, pass
slowly before the window.

"We children were brought up in the strict Calvin-
istic Church : it was rather the effect of practice and
example, than of much talk. The Lutherans of our
little town I used to regard as strangers, with whom I
must not be thoroughly familiar; and of the Catholics,
— who were always to be recognized by their gayer
dress, — I had a strange sort of dread. And I still feel
as if I could not be thoroughly devout anywhere but in

the church fitted up with the simplicity of the reformed faith; so strongly does all belief attach to the first impressions of childhood.

"Love of country was deeply impressed upon our hearts, I know not how, for of that, too, little was said; but there was nothing in our parents' lives or conversation which could suggest any other thought: we held our prince for the best in the world, our country for the most favored of all countries."

And yet this was only a very few years after that cruel sale of so many Hessian soldiers to be slaughtered in battle; and Jacob Grimm was born in the very year — 1785 — in which Frederic II. died.

But why do I talk of the Grimms? Only because these two brothers, of whom I have spoken, gathered together, from old libraries, and peasants' talk, and search in every quarter — through years of inquiry — a most famous collection of old nursery tales, fairy legends, and household stories.

And you would be surprised, if you were to read them through (which I cannot advise), to find how many of our old English stories, which we always thought must have had their beginning in England, were known still earlier, and gave joy and terror to young people ages ago, — before ever the present English language was known. Thus "Goody Two Shoes," and "Cinderella," and "Jack the Giant-Killer," and "Little Red Riding Hood," have all had their run among the young folks of older countries — centuries before such books were printed by "good Mr. Newbery," in St. Paul's Churchyard, in London. There are elves and giants, and good spirits and bad spirits, and

talking birds, and singing beasts, doing all manner of
wondrous things, in these books of the Grimm brothers.

But you must not think, that, because the brothers
Grimm were hunting after child's stories so toilsomely,
they were men of no learning. They were, in fact,
most wise and studious men, and are known among
scholars as the authors of very valuable works relating
to the German language, to which they devoted years of

A Trio.

labor. A son of William — the younger brother — was
asked one day, by a playmate, about his father's "fairy
stories." The boy was indignant, and on getting home,
said, " Surely, — surely, papa, you never can have written such rubbish. "

And is it rubbish ?

I suppose it must be said — begging young readers
who still love Tom Thumb, and Bo-peep, to pardon me

—that it is in one sense rubbish; just as you count dolls and Noah's arks rubbish, when you have outgrown such toys. But what if you could make a collection of all the best dolls and toys and games which have amused the children of six centuries past? Do you not think it would tell you a great deal you would like to know about the art, the skill, the material resources, and the home life of the people who lived so long ago?

And so these stories — however much nonsense may be in them — throw light upon the language and the domestic habits and the tastes of bygone nations; and they show how some strange traditions have held place from age to age; and how certain old stories of elves, or giants, or fairies, or goblins have kept life in them, when great schemes of philosophy that grew up beside them have died, and gone out of remembrance.

For such reasons these studious German brothers gave great care and labor to that collection of household stories, into the pages of which you shall now take a peep with me.

The Gold Bird.

A king had a garden where golden apples grew; but, as they became ripe, one of them was stolen every night. The king was angry; and the gardener set his sons to watch — turn by turn. The oldest, on his night, fell asleep; the second also fell asleep when his turn came; but the youngest son found that a gold bird stole them, and he fired upon it with his bow (of course there were no shot-guns), and cut away a golden feather from the robber.

A Ride on the Fox's Tail.

This was shown to the king, who found it so beautiful that he said he must have the bird.

Then the gardener sent his sons in search of the bird,
turn by turn, again. The oldest set off, and met a fox ;
and the fox said to him (for foxes could talk, and cats
could paint pictures, in that time), " You are after the
Golden Bird — I know : when you have walked all day
you will come to two inns — one on either side of the
road ; go into the poorest one, and you will fare best in
your search."

But the boy did not like the squat, small inn, where
he had been advised to go, but, entering the other, had
a jolly time there, and forgot the bird, and forgot his
home, and all at home forgot him.

Then the second son set off ; and *he* met the fox, and
did not like his talk, and shot an arrow at him. He
chose the best-looking inn, and had a jolly time ; and he
forgot the bird, and the king forgot him, and he forgot
his home.

Then the youngest son went on the search, though the
gardener was much afraid that harm would come to him
too. This son met the fox, but he listened patiently
to Renard ; and, as he was tired, the fox gave him a
seat upon his tail (as you see in the picture, which was
made from one of George Cruikshank's famous designs) ;
and away he went, with his hair whistling in the wind.

Of course he minded the fox, and stopped at the
humble-looking inn : he was not proud like the others.
In the morning the fox met him, and told him he must
go all day till he came to a castle, in the courts of
which castle the soldiers would be all asleep ; he must
not wake them, but go through the corridors of the

But the lazy sons, who went to the wrong inn, and would not listen to the wise words of the fox, waylaid him, and beat him, and took his treasures, and threw him in the river.

But the fox gave him a lift with his bushy tail, and he came to shore once more, and went whisking away to the kingdom of the golden apples. And when his story was told (I dare say the fox made it up for him), the lazy, lying brothers were put out of the way, and the plodding, straightforward, humble brother got his princess, and his horse, and his bird ; and, having given the bird to the king, he had the princess for his own, and lived very charmingly with her. He did not forget his good friend the fox, whom he met one day in the wood shortly after ; and the fox entreated him to cut off his (the fox's) head and tail.

He hesitated a long while ; but, after talking it over with the princess, he did as the fox desired. And what do you suppose happened then ? Why, the fox changed into a man — tall and comely, and in a royal purple suit ; and he turned out to be an own brother of the princess, who had been lost many years before.

I suppose he lived with the married pair, and used to talk with them of the old days when he was a fox, — just as retired merchants talk of the old days when they were "in trade."

More Queer Beasts and People.

I cannot tell you of one-half the queer things told in these books of old German tales, so I must skip about from page to page. In one, for instance, I catch sight of a fox tied by his fore-paws to the branches of two trees. How, pray, did this come about? The story says that a wolf, and a fox, and a rabbit, were bent on learning to play the violin, and begged a musician to teach them.

The Three Musicians.

He promised to do so, if they would obey orders. So, walking through the wood with them, he ordered the wolf to put his paws in the crack of a tree—which he did ; and was made fast there—at his lesson. A little farther on, he bent down two boughs, and ordered the fox to place a paw on each, where the musician tied them fast, and left the fox—to his lesson. A little farther on, he bound the rabbit by a silken string to a tree-trunk, where he presently, by bouncing about, wound himself fast—to his lesson. I suppose they all commenced squeaking and howling, each in his own way—which happens to a great many who commence the study of music.

They worried out of their fastenings at last, and came on fast and furious to attack the musician — who had meantime taught a man that understood what music meant, and who defended his master, as he should. The beasts had the worst of it.   I don't know what the moral of it is — unless that animals who have no ear for music should always keep to their howling and squealing, and never attack a good musician — whose melody they cannot equal, and whose merit they cannot know.

I espy, too, among the hobgoblins, little English Red Riding Hood, or Red-cap as they call her, seated on the German ground, with her basket and her pretty ways; and I find there is a new reading to her story.

Little Red-cap.

The wolf comes for her — drops soft speeches in her ear — but she doubts him: she goes to her grand-mamma with her comfits, and tells her how the wolf tried to mislead her.

Then the great wolf comes croaking to the door:

he has fine gifts for Grandmamma; he will be good:
Riding Hood shall have fine dresses.

But no : Grandmamma is stern, and keeps the door
shut. The wolf climbs upon the roof — watching and
waiting, and waiting —

When little Red-cap comes out he will snatch her.
But Grandmamma bethinks herself of some savory
water she has ; and she and Red-cap fill a great trough
with it, outside the door. The wolf scents, and sniffs,
and sniffs, and slips down and down, and stretches his
neck to reach it — lower and lower — till at last, off he
goes — souse — into the trough, and is drowned there —
as all prowling wolves should be who would devour
sweet little Red-caps.

The Elves.

I meet with hosts of little elves who come by moonlight and in the dark, and dance on the greensward, and
hang upon tree-boughs as if they grew there, and bustle
around babies' cradles, whispering so softly, in baby's
ear, that nurse never hears them. They tease selfish cur-
mudgeons ; and they help, with the daintiest of fingers,

a poor cobbler who is reduced to his last bit of leather: they transform themselves into awl and hammer, and work all through the night, making better shoes than the cobbler ever could have made; and he receives double price for their work, and grows prosperous.

Mr. Cruikshank has made a delicious picture of the old cobbler and his wife peeping from behind the door at night, to see these little elves frolicking around his bench, and putting on the gay clothes the cobbler's wife has made for the little helpers. The elves put on the new clothes, indeed; but then they dashed away, and were heard of no more.

We talk, you know, about being in "good spirits," or in "bad spirits." I think those old Germans who made these stories would have said instead — the good elves have come; or the bad elves have come. The good elves will stay, — unless we try to dress them up unnaturally, and extravagantly fine. As for the bad ones, — if we never hunt after them at night, or feed them with high-spiced dishes, — they will go.

The Flower with a Pearl.

One other story I must tell, of a bad fairy — a hag, in fact — who lived in a great grim castle. By night she became an owl; by day she was sometimes a cat, with her back in a rounded arch. If young girls went within a hundred paces of her castle walls, they were changed into nightingales, which the bad fairy caught, and hung in cages in a certain chamber of her castle. If young men came within a hundred paces, they too had a spell upon them, so that they could not move except the cruel fairy waved her wand, and bade them begone.

Now, Jorinda and Jorindel — who were young people
of that region — loved each other dearly, and knew all
about the fairy ; but yet, as lovers will, they wandered out
by moonlight, without knowing how far they were going.
Jorinda was singing sweetly, —

> " The ring-dove sang from the willow spray, —
> Well-a-day ! well-a-day !
> He mourned for the fate
> Of his lovely mate :
> Well-a-day ! " ———

Jorindel was listening, as lovers will ; and for a time
did not know that they had come too near the bad
fairy's walls, and that Jorinda was changed, and he was
listening only to a nightingale. He saw a dreadful owl
flit by ; and at dawn, lo ! — there came the dreadful fairy
with her cloak, and her staff, and her cage, and her nose
and chin almost touching, and carried off Jorinda. He
could not stir to help her, you know ; and, if he could,
— how was he to help a nightingale ?

Then the hag waved her wand, and bade him begone.
He begged and pleaded ; but all the more her nose and
chin came clacking together, and all the more she bade
him begone.

In despair he went and became a shepherd — listening in the fields at night for the songs of the nightingales, who reminded him of his darling Jorinda.

At last, one night he dreamed — that in the meadows
he found a scarlet flower, with a pearl in the middle of
it ; and that with this flower he marched straight up to
the walls of the fairy's castle, and that at a touch of
his flower the gates sprang open, and that he saw his
own Jorinda again.

Next day he hunted to find if such a flower grew in those meadows. He hunted long, — day after day, — and at last found the treasure. He went straightway — though the journey was long — to the castle of the cruel old woman. And, sure enough, at a touch of the flower the gates swung wide open. In he went, through corridor after corridor, till at last he heard the singing

Jorindel touches the Cage.

nightingales; and, in the room where seven hundred cages were hanging, was the wicked fairy with her staff. She was mad with rage, but the flower protected him.

He looked around to find Jorinda; for, lover as he was, he did not want seven hundred Jorindas.

Meantime the wicked fairy — while her black cat was

bristling at Jorindel — was bustling out of the door. She had seized a cage to take with her. What if this were the very nightingale he wanted? He rushed after her; he touched the cage with his magic flower, and lo! the tender Jorinda, beautiful as ever, stood before him.

Of course they embraced, as lovers — after a long separation — should. Then Jorindel set all the other nightingales free; and the great troop of beautiful girls marched out of the castle, and the bad fairy was neither found nor heard of again.

It was a good thing for Jorinda that she had a lover who was constant, and who could find a flower with a pearl in it.

IX.

A SCOTCH MAGICIAN.

Ivanhoe.

I DON'T think I shall ever forget my first reading of Scott's story of "Ivanhoe"—not if I live to be as old as Dr. Parr.

It was about the time when I was half through Adams's Latin Grammar (which nobody studies now). I was curled up in an easy-chair, with one of those gilt-backed volumes in my hand, which made a long array in a little upstairs book-case of a certain stone house that fronts the sea. Snowing, I think, and promising good sliding down hill (we knew nothing about any such word as "coasting" in those days). But snow and sleds and mittens were all forgotten in that charming story, where I saw old Saxon England, and the brave Cœur de Lion who was king, and a pretty princess, and dashing men-at-arms, and heard clash of battle, and bugle notes, and prayerful entreaties of a sweet Jewess, and anthems in old abbeys.

All these so lingered in my mind, that when, years

after, I went rambling through England, I wandered one day all around the town of Ashby-de-la-Zouche to find —if it might be found — the old tournament-ground where was held the famous fête that opens so grandly the story of "Ivanhoe;" and, in going through Sherwood Forest (what is left of it), I think the Robin Hood of Scott's story was as lively in my thought as the Robin Hood of the old ballads.

And now the story must be told over in a few pages. A few pages! Ah, there was a time when I wished the two hundred pages could be stretched into five hundred! I hear the young people of our day complain that they can't like the long talks and the long descriptions; and that Scott's books are too slow for them. Well, well! I know that the day of chivalry, and of men-at-arms, and "knights caparisoned," is gone by; but there are old heads into which the din of those gone-by times does come at odd intervals, floating musically, — and never so musically as on the pages of Scott. What if we try to whisk a little of this music into a page of story?

The first scene shows a swineherd, with rough jerkin; his tangled hair is his only cap, and a brass band is around his neck, and he is talking with the fool Wamba, who sits upon a bank in the forest. They are the serfs of an old Saxon named Cedric, who lives near by, in a great, sprawling, half-fortified country-house. And when Gurth, the swineherd, and Wamba go home at night, there is met a great company in the hall of Cedric, their master. A famous Templar knight, Sir Brian du Bois-Guilbert, is there with his retinue; and Cedric has seated by him Rowena, a beautiful princess, who is living under his guardianship; and there is a pilgrim from the Holy Land in the company, — who is a disguised knight (and the son of Cedric, but has been disinherited by the father because he has dared to love the beautiful Rowena); and there is a rich old white-bearded

Swineherd and Wamba.

Jew, — Isaac of York, — who is buffeted by the company, but who is richer than them all. The timber roof of the apartment is begrimed with smoke, that rises from a great fireplace at the end of the hall. Yet the meats are good, and there is wine and ale. There is talk of the battles of the Crusaders in Palestine, and of the valiant deeds of Richard the Lion-hearted, who is a prisoner (or thought to be) somewhere on the Continent; and there is talk, too, of the great tournament at Ashby, where all the company is going on the morrow.

But no one knows the secret of the disguised pilgrim, who at dawn next day steals out secretly,—taking Gurth with him, and telling the swineherd who he really is. He befriends the Jew too; and so, through his aid, procures a steed and new armor for the battle of the tournament.

The Tournament.

It was a gorgeous scene at Ashby. Prince John, the usurping king (brother to Richard), was there with his court, and Rowena—beautiful as ever; and still more beautiful was Rebecca, the "peerless daughter" of the Jew, Isaac of York. Of course there was, too, a great crowd of Saxon knights and of Norman barons, and of people of all degrees,—such a crowd, in short, as gathers at one of our great fairs or races. But remember that very few of the great people, even in this gathering of Richard Cœur de Lion's day, could write their own names; and it was a long time before there was any such thing in existence as a printed book. But yet I think the show of fine feathers and silks, and coquetry, was as great then as it would be in any such great assemblage now.

Well, in all the knightly sports of the early part of the day, Bois-Guilbert was easily chief; but before the day ended, a new knight made his appearance on the field, with visor down, unknown to all, and with only this

device on his shield, — a young oak torn up by the
roots, and the word " Disinherited." Everybody admired his motions and his carriage; and everybody
trembled when he rode bravely up to the tents of the
challengers, and smote the shield of Bois-Guilbert with
the point of his lance. This meant deadly strife; while,
before this time, all the combats had been with blunted
javelins.

A Strange Knight.

So the knights took up position, and at a blast from
the trumpets dashed forward into the middle of the
lists, and met with a shock that must have been a fearful thing to see. Neither was unhorsed, though the
lances of both were shattered in splinters. At the
second trial, Bois-Guilbert rolled over in the dust, and
the strange knight (whose real name was Ivanhoe) was
declared victor.

The air rang with shouts, and Ivanhoe rode around
the lists to single out a fair lady who should be queen

of the next day's fête. Of course he chose Rowena, the Saxon princess, who sat beside Athelstane, who was of royal Saxon blood and was her declared lover, and favored by Cedric, who sat also beside her.

But neither Cedric, nor Rowena, nor Prince John knew who the strange knight could be, since he had refused to lift the visor of his helmet, or to declare his name. The Jew, Isaac of York, doubtless knew the steed and the armor, and may have whispered what he knew to Rebecca; for when Ivanhoe at evening sent his man Gurth to pay the Jew for his equipments, the beautiful Rebecca detained the messenger at the door, and paid him back the money — and more; saying that so true and good a knight, who had befriended her father, owed him nothing.

Rebecca and the Messenger.

This was a most splendid thing for Rebecca to do, we all thought.

The next day, there was a little army on each side in the contest; Bois-Guilbert leading one, and Ivanhoe the other. For a long time the result was doubtful; but at

last Ivanhoe was beset by three knights at once, — Bois-
Guilbert, Athelstane, and Front de Bœuf; and surely
would have been conquered if a new party had not appeared. This was a gigantic knight in black armor,
with no device, and who had acted the sluggard. He
rode up at sight of Ivanhoe's sore need, and, with a
careless blow or two from mace or battle-axe, sent Front
de Bœuf and Athelstane reeling in the dust. After
this, the victory of Ivanhoe was easy and complete.

They led him up to receive the crown from Rowena,
the queen of the fête; and they unloosed his helmet,
though he made signs to them to forbear; and Cedric
knew his son, and Rowena knew her lover, and Prince
John knew the favorite of the wronged King Richard,
whose power he was usurping.

But the poor knight was wounded grievously; and,
taking off his corslet, the attendants found a spear-head
driven into his breast. And he was taken away to be
cared for, — none knew exactly by whom; but it appeared afterward that it was by those in the employ of
Rebecca, who, like many ladies of that day, was a great
mistress of the healing craft.

A Castle.

A day or two later, as I remember, he was journeying in a litter under care of the Jew and Rebecca,
who were attacked by outlaws; and, after this, claimed
the protection of Cedric and Athelstane, and their company, who also were journeying through the same region; but these latter did not know who was the
wounded man in the litter. Even if they had known,

they could not have protected him against the enemies who presently beset them ; for they all were taken captive, and lodged in the great castle of Front de Bœuf.

Ah, what a castle it was! What dungeons! What mysterious posterns! What embrasures, and courts, and turrets, and thick walls, and secret passages!

I see in one of its dungeons the old Jew, appealing to Front de Bœuf, who threatens to draw out his teeth one

Front de Bœuf and the Jew.

by one, or to roast him by the dungeon fire, if he will not disgorge his money.

I see Rebecca, beautiful and defiant, wooed by Bois-Guilbert as captives are always wooed by conquerors, until with proud daring she threatens to throw herself from the embrasure of the window, headlong down the walls.

I see Ivanhoe stretched upon his sick-couch, helpless,

and listening yearningly to the sounds that come up from the castle walls. I see the beautiful Rebecca — who is in attendance upon him (we boys were all so glad of that !) — exposing herself to chance arrows from Robin Hood's band, who are attacking the castle, only that she may look out and report to the poor knight Ivanhoe how the battle is going. She says a giant in black armor is heading the attacking party, and that he thunders with his great battle-axe upon the postern gate as if the might of an army were in his hand. She says the men go down under his strokes as if God's lightning had smitten them. He knows who it must be. It is — it can be no other than the Black Sluggard of the tournament — Richard I. of England !

"Look again, Rebecca."

"God of Abraham ! They are toppling over a great stone from the battlements; it must crush the brave knight !"

Poor Ivanhoe ! Poor captives !

"But no, he is safe ; he is thundering at the gate ; it splinters under his blows ! Ah, the blood ! the trampled men ! Great God ! are these thy children ?"

Yet even now there are inner and higher walls of the castle to be climbed or battered down. Never would they have been taken except there had been treachery within. A wretched woman — Ulrica, victim of Front de Bœuf — has set a match to a great store of fuel, and smoke and flame belch out : the defenders have fires to fight, and their outposts are weakened ; and the attacking party press on, and secure the citadel. I seem to see smoke and flame, and crushing towers, under whose ruins lie buried Front de Bœuf and the miserable Ulrica.

I see Cedric disguised as priest, and making his escape, and flinging back bribes in scorn.

Then, upon a patch of greensward under the shadow of a near grove of oaks, the victors gather slowly to measure their spoil.

The Saxon Rowena is safe — so is the Jew and Cedric. Athelstane has received what seems his death-

Cedric disguised as Priest.

wound. Ivanhoe has been snatched out of the jaws of destruction by the arm of King Richard, who bids Cedric be reconciled with his son; which bidding, the old Saxon curmudgeon cannot deny; and he is half disposed — now that the royal lover Athelstane is out of the way — to favor the pretensions of Ivanhoe to the hand and heart of Rowena. Robin Hood, in his suit of green, gets free grace for all his misdeeds as outlaw, and with one of his "merry men,"—a certain jolly friar of Copmanhurst, who does not know the secret of the Black Knight, — the easy-going, stalwart king has a sparring-match (which to every boy reader of our time was delightful) ; and which ended with putting the great jolly friar sprawling in the dirt. What a brave, stout king was Richard, to be sure !

But the only real grief among all who have been res-cued is shown by the poor old Jew — not so much for the moneys which the barons and the church people have shorn him of, as for his daughter. The sweet Rebecca has not been crushed, indeed, in the ruin of the castle ; but she has been borne away a captive by a knight who was none other than the wicked Templar, Bois-Guilbert. Whither, none knew ; nor does the story of her seizure come to the ears of Ivanhoe (for which, I fear, Row-ena was glad), who is borne away to some religious house, where he will have more orthodox, — though not more gentle care than the tender Rebecca would have rendered.

After this, I seem to see a great crowd of mourners in some old monastery or religious house of some sort, bewailing (with good eating and flagons of ale) the lost Athelstane ; and in the middle of the funeral feast — which the king had honored with his presence, and Rowena, and the knight Ivanhoe — lo! Athelstane him-self, with his grave-clothes on him, suddenly appears ! Good old Walter Scott loved such surprises as he loved a good dinner. The royal Saxon lover of Rowena was not really dead, but had only been stunned by a fearful blow. But the blow has cleared his brain, and made him see that Rowena cares more for the little finger of

Ivanhoe than for his whole body; so he tells Cedric he gives up his claim.

And what does Ivanhoe say?

There is no Ivanhoe to be found. A mysterious messenger has summoned him away; and, though scarce able to sit his horse for his sore wounds, he has put on his armor, and dashed through the outlying forests. He rides hard, and he rides fast, for there is a dear life at stake. Whose?

(If we were writing a novel, we should say "CHAPTER SECOND" here, and make a break. Then we should begin ——)

Rebecca.

We return now to Rebecca. Bois-Guilbert had indeed borne her away, and had lodged her in a great house that belonged to the Knights Templars. But the Grand Master of the Templars, to whom Bois-Guilbert owed obedience, was a very severe man, and a very curious, prying man; and he found out speedily what Bois-Guilbert had done; and he found out that this young woman, beautiful as she was, was a Jewess; and there were some among the Templars who said she was a sorceress too, and had practised her sorcery upon Bois-Guilbert. So this Grand Master of the Templars brought the poor girl to trial for sorcery, though she was the most Christian and most lovable creature in the whole book!

It was a sorry, sham trial: the Templars all on one side, and the poor Jewess on the other; — for the miserable fellow, Bois-Guilbert, was afraid to open his mouth

in her defence. He told her, indeed, that he would
save her, and run off with her if she would go ; but she
scorned him with a most brave and beautiful scorn.
Of course she came off badly at the trial, — as they
meant she should. She was condemned to be burned.
Only one chance for escape was left, — she might sum-
mon a knight to her defence, who must contend against
the bravest and strongest of the Templars. If her champion won, she might go free ; if he failed by a hair's
breadth, the fagots would be kindled around her.

But who would defend a Jewess? Who would be
champion for a suspected sorceress ?

She craved the privilege of sending out a messenger,
in faint hope of finding a champion. And the messenger rode — a good fellow — rode fast, rode far ; 'twas he
that found Ivanhoe, and 'twas with him that the good
knight left the scene of Athelstane's coming to life.

The morning came. The fagots were piled up ; the
match-fire was ready ; the Templars were all gathered ;
the stout Brien du Bois-Guilbert, armed *cap-à-pie*, was
ready for any champion ; the great warning-bell began
tolling — One ! two ! three ———

What dust is that rising yonder? It is — it is a
knight — in full armor ; he approaches — he comes in
plain sight. It is Ivanhoe ; but ah ! so weak, so wearied,
so wasted by his sickness ! There is but little hope for
poor Rebecca. But he enters the lists ; he braves the
challenger ; the trumpet sounds ; the steeds dash away
to the encounter, and the crash of meeting comes.

The Grand Master strains his eyes to see what figures
shall come out from the cloud of dust. One is down, —
prostrate utterly, — dying. Of course it must be the

Rebecca's Trial.

enfeebled and fatigued Ivanhoe. But no — no — it is
not! It is Bois-Guilbert who is dying.

And what is this new cloud of dust and tramp of cav-
alry? It is Richard of England, who has followed hard
upon the track of Ivanhoe; for he has heard of his errand, and knows he is unfit to encounter the strongest
of the Templar Knights. He has brought a squadron
of armed men with him, too, to seize upon all traitors in

The Champion.

the ranks of the Templars; and lo! above the roof and
towers of the Grand Master of the Templars, the royal
standard of England is even now floating in the breeze.
And Rebecca is safe, and Ivanhoe is safe.

And did he marry her?

Ah, no! He married the Saxon Rowena; and they
had a grand wedding in York Minster, where now you
may see the pavement on which they walked.

One day after the wedding, — it may have been a

week later, — a visitor asked an interview with the
bride. The visitor was a closely veiled lady of most
graceful figure. You guess who it was, — Rebecca.
She brought a gift for the bride of Ivanhoe, — a gorgeous necklace of diamonds, — so magnificent that
Rowena felt like refusing the gift.

"I pray you take them, dear lady," said Rebecca.
"I owe this, and more, to the good knight, — your
honored " — Here she broke down ; but she recovered
herself presently — kissed the hand of Rowena — passed
out.

I think Rowena was glad her visitor did not meet
Ivanhoe upon the stairs ; I think she was glad, too, that
the lovely Rebecca went over seas presently to Spanish
Granada ; though she pretended not to be.

I know if *I* had been Ivanhoe —— But we will not
try to mend a story of Scott's ; least of all, when we
crowd one of his novels into a few pages, as we have
done here.

Walter Scott's Home.

It is among the very earliest recollections of my
school-days, — that the master, after some exercise in
reading, told us youngsters — with a grave face — that
the great author Sir Walter Scott was dead. And I
think some lout of a boy down the bench — with a big
shock of hair, and who was a better hand at marbles
than he ever was at books — said, in a whisper that
two or three of us caught, — "I wonder who under the
canopy *he* was ?"

I don't think that, for any of us, Scott was so large a

man, in that time, as Peter Parley, — who, if I remember rightly, was at about that date writing his little square books of "Travels" in strange lands.

It was at a later day that we boys began to catch the full flavor of Waverley, and the Heart of Mid-Lothian, and of that glorious story of battles and single-handed fights in which the gallant Saladin and the ponderous Richard of the Lion Heart took part. We may possibly have read at that tender age his "Tales of a Grandfather" (which will make good reading for young people now) ; and we may have heard our lady kinsfolk talk admiringly of the Lady of the Lake, and of Marmion ; but we did not measure fairly the full depth of the school-master's grave manner, when he told us, in 1832, that Walter Scott was dead.

For my part, when I did get into the full spirit of Guy Mannering and of Ivanhoe, some years later, it seemed to me a great pity that a man who could make such books should die at all, — and a great pity that he should not go on writing them to the latest generation of men. And I do not think that I had wholly shaken off this feeling, when I wandered twelve years later along the Tweed, — looking sharply out in the Scotch mist that drifted among the hollows of the hills, for the gray ruin of Melrose Abbey.

I knew that this beautiful ruin was near to the old homestead of Walter Scott, toward which I had set off on a foot pilgrimage, a day before, from the old border-town of Berwick-upon-Tweed. If you have read any Scottish history, or if you have read Miss Porter's great story (as we boys thought it) of "The Scottish Chiefs," you will have heard of this old border-town.

I had kept close along the banks of the river, — seeing
men drawing nets for salmon, — seeing charming fields
green with the richest June growth, — seeing shepherds
at sheep-washing on Tweedside, — seeing old Norham
Castle, and Coldstream Bridge, and the palace of the
Duke of Roxburgh. I had slept at Kelso, — had
studied the great bit of ruin which is there, and had
caught glimpses of Teviotdale, and of the Eildon Hills ;
I had dined at a drover's inn of St. Boswell's ; I had
trudged out of my way for a good look at Smaillholme
Tower, and at the farmhouse of Sandy Knowe — both
which you will find mention of, if you read (as you
should) Lockhart's Life of Scott. Dryburgh Abbey,
with its gloom, and rich tresses of ivy vines, — where
the great writer lies buried, — came later in the day ;
and at last, in the gloaming (which is the pretty Scotch
word for twilight), a stout oarsman ferried me across a
stream, and I toiled foot-sore into the little town of Melrose. There is not much to be seen there but the
Abbey in its ghostly ruin. I slept at the George Inn,
dreaming — as I dare say you would have done — of
Ivanhoe, Rebecca, and border wars and Old Mortality.

Next morning, after a breakfast upon trout which had
been taken from some near stream (was it the Yarrow ?)
I strolled two miles or so down the road, and by a little
green foot-gate entered upon the grounds of Abbotsford — which was the home that Walter Scott created,
and the home where he died.

The forest trees — not over-high at that time — under
which I walked were those which he had planted. I
found his favorite out-of-door seat, — sheltered by a
thicket of arbor-vitæ trees, — from which there could

be caught a glimpse of the rippled surface of the Tweed, and a glimpse of the many turrets which crowned the house of Abbotsford.

It was all very quiet ; quiet in the walks through the wide-stretching wood ; and quiet as you came to the court-yard and doorway of the beautiful house. I think there was a yelp from some young hound in an out-building ; there was a little twitter from some birds I did not know with my American eyes ; there was the pleasant and unceasing murmur of the river, rustling over its broad, pebbly bed. Beside these sounds the silence was unbroken ; and when I rang the bell at the entrance door, the echoes of it fairly startled me,— and they startled a little terrier too, whose quick, sharp bark rang noisily through the outer court of the great building.

This seemed very dismal. Where, pray, were Tom Purdy, and Laidlaw, and Maida, and Sibyl Gray? For you must remember I was, in that day, fresh from a first reading of Lockhart's Life of Scott, in which all these — and many more — appear, and give life and stir to the surroundings of this home of Abbotsford.

You will read that book of Lockhart's some day, and you will find in it — that Tom Purdy was an old out-of-door servant of Scott's, who looked after the plantation and the dogs, and always accompanied the master upon his hunting frolics and his mountain strolls. Laidlaw did service in a more important way in-doors, — reading and writing for the master of the house. Maida was a noble stag-hound, whom Scott loved almost as much as any creature about him, and of whom he has left a charming portrait in old " Bevis," — whose acquaintance

you will make whenever you come to read the tale of
" Woodstock." As for Sibyl Gray, it was the name
of the stout nag which carried Scott safely through
fords and fens.

But, as I said, there were none of them to be seen on
that morning — thirty odd years ago — at Abbotsford.
I could not even be sure that the terrier which set up
so shrill and discordant a barking belonged to that
sharp " Mustard " family, which traces back to Dandie
Dinmont's home in Guy Mannering.

Only an old housekeeper was in charge ; who, though
she might have seen service in the family, had fallen
into that parrot-like way of telling visitors what things
were best worth seeing, that frets one terribly who goes
to such a place with the memory of old stories glow-
ing in his thought. What would you or I care, —
fresh from Ivanhoe, —whether a certain bit of carving
came from Jedburgh, or from Kelso ? What should we
care about the number of jets in the chandelier in the
great hall ? What should we care about the way in
which Prince Somebody — wrote his name in the visitors' book ?

But when we catch sight of the desk at which the master wrote, or of the chair in which he sat, and of his
shoes, and coat, and cane, — looking as if they might
have been worn only yesterday, — this seems to bring
us nearer to the man who has written so much to cheer
and charm the world. There was too, I remember, a
little box in the corridor, — simple and iron-bound, —
with the line written below it, — " Post will close at
two."

It was as if we had heard the master of the house say
it to a guest, — " The post will close at two."

Perhaps the notice was in his own handwriting, — perhaps not ; yet somehow, more than the library, more than the portrait bust of the dead author, — more than all the chatter of the well-meaning housekeeper, — it brought back the halting old gentleman in his shooting-coat, and with his ivory-headed cane, — hobbling with a vigorous pace along the corridor, to post in that old iron-bound box a chapter — maybe, of Ivanhoe.

The Chair, Coat, and Cane.

But no : Ivanhoe was written before this great pile of Abbotsford was finished. Indeed, the greater part of his best work was done under a roof much more homely and modest, — perhaps at a farmhouse he once occupied some miles away on the Esk, — perhaps in the humbler building which was overbuilt and swamped in this great pile of masonry.

It is not old, as you may think: it has a vexing
look of newness for those who love his tales of the
Covenanters.   Of course it was more vexing thirty-three
years ago than now; but even now, if you go there,
— and all who go to Scotland are tempted to run down
over that thirty miles of distance which separates it
from Edinboro', — you will still find none of the venerable oldness, which — going from our new country —
we love to meet.

The walls and halls of that house of Abbotsford are
fine; but there are far finer ones to be seen in England
and Scotland.   I do not know what mosses may have
grown over it during these thirty-three years last past,
to make it venerable; but — that number of years ago,
it wore a showy newness that was quite shocking to one
that had learned to think (from his books) that dear old
Walter Scott should have lived all his life sheltered by
a mossy roof, and by walls mellowed in their hue by the
storms, and stains, and suns of centuries.

I found no whit of this about Abbotsford.   You
know, I dare say, that it had been only a little while his
home at the time of his death: only twice after its
completion had all the great rooms been thrown open,
— once when his son Capt. Walter Scott, of the Royal
Hussars, was married to a Highland heiress; and again
when Sir Walter Scott, baronet and author, lay in state
there, and the house was thronged with mourners.

Its turrets and great stretch of courts and corridors
and halls tell a mournful story of that weak ambition in
him which sought to dignify in this way a great family
pride.   It was an ambition that was not gratified in his
lifetime; and now there is not one of his lineage or
name to hold possession of it.

How and When He wrote.

It is not so very long ago that Scott wrote his charming stories : — since Goldsmith — long since Dr. Swift — since Miss Edgeworth made her fame (though he died before she died) ; indeed, he is nearer to our times than any I have spoken of, or shall speak of, in this budget of " Old Story-Tellers." There are those alive who remember well the great mystery about the Waverley Novels ; — for, while everybody was reading them, nobody could say certainly who wrote them.

Scott did not place his name upon the title-page of these books ; he did not allow it to be known for years — even among his intimate friends — who wrote them. There were those who went to his home, and staid there day after day, — joining him in his rambles over the gray hills, — listening to his dinner tales, and the snatches of old songs he loved to recite, — who said it could never be Walter Scott, who wrote the tales at which the world was wondering ; for what time could such a man find for such amazing work ?

But there were keener ones who noted that the master of the house never, or very rarely, showed himself to his guests until after ten in the morning ; and between that hour and sunrise — at which time he rose — those who were most familiar with him knew that this wonderful work was done. Never, I suppose, did any literary man work more rapidly. Writing thus, and aiming only at those broad effects which enchanted the whole world of readers, — he could not and did not give that close attention to his sentences which Goldsmith and Swift both gave, and which makes their writings far safer and better as models of style. He wrote so swiftly, and dashed so strongly into the current of what he had to say, that he was careless about every thing except what went to engage the reader, and enchain his attention.

But do you say that this is the very best aim of all writing? Most surely it is wise for a writer to seek to engage attention; and failing of this, he must fail of any further purpose; but if he gains this by simple means, — by directness, — by clear, limpid language, and no more words than the thought calls for — and such rhythmic and beguiling use of them as tempts the reader to keep all in mind, he is a safer example to follow than one who, by force of genius, can bring into large use extravagant expressions, and great redundance of words.

Scott has in one of his stories — "The Talisman " — an account of a trial of prowess between Saladin, the Eastern monarch, and our old friend, Richard the Lion-hearted. They are together somewhere on one of those fairy islets of green, which are scattered over the sandy wastes of Palestine. The subjects of both monarchs are gathered together: there is peace between them for the time; they mingle in friendly games. The great Saxon king — that is, Richard — wishes to astonish and impress those light-limbed warriors of the East: so he takes a great iron mace, or, as we might say, a solid iron bludgeon, and lays it upon a block which he has ordered to be brought into the presence of Saladin and his attendant chieftains. Then he raises his great two-handed broad-sword, — not over-sharp, but immensely heavy, — and, sweeping it through the air, brings it down with a mighty thwack upon the iron bludgeon, which straightway falls clanging in two pieces, — cleft apart by the force of the king's blow.

The light cimeter and the light arm of Saladin can do no such thing as this: the men of Palestine know it; the British warriors — looking on — all know it, and cannot keep down a shout of triumph.

What then does Saladin, — whose turn to show his prowess has now come? He can cleave no iron mace: he looks upon the cleft bludgeon with as much wonder as any. He tests coolly the edge of his cimeter: he knows its keenness; he knows what swiftness and surety he can give to its sweep. He takes a scarf of silken gauze — so fine that spiders might have woven it, — so light, it seems to float on the air, as the Saladin tosses it from him. Then — quick as lightning, he draws his cimeter — strikes at the silken gauze, and the scarf, cleanly divided, drifts in two parcels down the wind.

Though we may admire almost evenly (as Scott meant we should) these feats of hand, it is certain we could never approach the doughty doing of Richard unless we were possessed of his gigantic power of muscle; but skill and practice would bring one to a very close approach to the deft accomplishment of Saladin.

Now, why have I brought in this little side-scene from the Talisman? You must remember that I was talking of words and style. Do you see now my intent? A man of genius — well informed as to his subject-matter, and full of enthusiasm — may be sure of triumph, through whatever cumbersome welter of words;

but a better example for you and for me to study, will be the work of one who gained his victories by simple, clear-cut sentences, that carry no burden of repetitions, and strike straight and sharp to the mark.

His Life and Ways.

But how came this man to write at all? His father, who was a quiet old gentleman in Edinburgh, believed

The boy Walter Scott.

and hoped that this son Walter would keep on with him in that steady office-work — it was of a legal sort — in which he himself grew old. He had fears indeed, when Walter was a boy, that he would slip from life early; for he had a grievous illness that left him a crippled man always, — not indeed badly crippled, but with a slight limp in his walk, which made his cane a thing of real service to him. He was a well-looking boy, — as you may see from this little picture of him in his childhood ; and much of his time was passed with his grandparents and relatives out by Kelso, or Sandy Knowe ; and I think he grew into a love for that region, and for all of Teviotdale, and Tweedside, which he never outgrew.

He did put himself to work, when the time came for it, in the office of his father ; but he did not bring a strong love for it.

He had read ballads out at Sandy Knowe, and had listened to old wives' tales, — in those days of his illness, — which stuck by him ; and the Eildon Hills, and the blue line of the Cheviots, I dare say kept coming into view, over his desk in Castle Street, Edinburgh.

There were young fellows too in the city — friends of his — who loved the heather, and border tales, and old lore, as well as he ; and we may be sure they had their junketings together, and that the legal work was none the better for it. There were certain ballads in their times, translated from the German, so daintily done, that they passed from hand to hand among the literary people of Edinburgh ; and the story ran that the pretty and musical translations were the work of Walter Scott, — a presentable young man, of some six feet in height, with a tall forehead, and bushy eyebrows, and a limp in his gait.

Then came a volume or two of collected Scottish minstrelsy, — much of the best work in them known to have been done by the same Walter Scott, and published with his name.

It did not help the law business ; and when a jingling, charming poem, full of the spirit of old balladry, and called "The Lay of the Last Minstrel," appeared under his name, it hurt the law business still more ; and we may well believe that the old gentleman — his father — shook his head despairingly.

But he received five or six hundred pounds for it, — which was better worth than two or three years of his law work.

Still, he tells us, he hesitated: should he give up rhyme-making, and keep close to his office ?

Well, if he had done so, we might possibly have had the Decisions of Justice Scott, in law calf; but should we have had "Ivanhoe"?

His poems had a taking, jingling resonance, and a fire, and a dash, and bold rich painting of Scotch scenery in them, that made them the delight of all England and Scotland. Everybody talked of the young Mr. Scott.

He married in this time a pretty Miss Carpenter, who was the orphan daughter of a French mother, and under the guardianship of Lord Downshire. This was very much against the wish of the elder Scotts. They were too old-fashioned to think well of French blood. But I believe she made a good wife, though she never got over her broken English, and always had over-due respect for titles ; and never, I think, had full and deep sympathy with the higher impulses of the great Scotch-man, or any wise appreciation of his best work. Per-haps I ought not to say this : certainly there was never any lack of that affection, on both sides, which is, after all, the thing that is most sure to make lasting domestic happiness.

Scott's poems are not yet, I think, wholly gone by. Marmion and the Lady of the Lake are still read, and are worth the reading, were it only for their charming glimpses of Scotch landscape; and if you ever go to Inversnaid and Loch Katrine, or sleep at one of the little ivy-embowered inns among the Trosachs, or look off from the heights of Stirling Castle, — you will be glad these old poems are still printed, and that you have read them. And, if you never visit those places, a reading of the poems will almost carry you there.

But Mr. Scott could not go on making poems forever: he had lifted all the blinding mists from those charming Scotch lakes; but when he carried his eight-syllabled music — which was ringing in everybody's ears — to England and " Rokeby," there was a pause in the welcomes that had greeted him. Besides, Byron had begun *his* chant in a new and more brilliant strain.

There was wisdom in his decision to strike a new note in Waverley, and Guy Mannering, — a note that is ringing yet. The clash of Marmion we only catch the hearing of here and there, at long intervals; but it is very hard, I think, to go where you will not meet those who know Dominie Samson, and Meg Merrilies.

Do you ask what I would counsel you to read among these novels of Scott?

Well — well! Does the maple, or the ash, or the pepperidge, or the dogwood show a richer color in autumn? Which of these shall we gather? which shall we leave ungathered?

Whatever else you may, or may not do, in the reading of Scott, I say — by all means read Old Mortality; read Waverley; read Guy Mannering; read the Heart of

Mid-Lothian; read Ivanhoe; and if you would be in weeping mood, and sigh over distresses you cannot help, — read the Bride of Lammermoor.

I have told you that Scott was not for a long time known as the author of these tales, — save to a few of his most intimate friends; and the full story of it was only noised widely, and to all the world, when his fortune broke down under the weight of Johnny Ballantyne's recklessness, and Constables' (his publishers) canny self-seeking, and the costs of that great pile of Abbotsford, and of the profitless moorlands he had with a strange ambition heaped together about his home.

All this brought age to him, and blight. He struggled bravely indeed; he wrote in this time of breaking hopes that charming story of Woodstock.

But he fought at very hard odds the battle of life, after this. Great earnings were small, compared with the great debts that shadowed him.

Death came too, into his new and splendid home: Charlotte, his wife, the companion of so many years, died. The tragedy of Lammermoor will not touch you more than the story of this grief, as he has written it down in a few swift, crazy words, in his Diary.

After this, the wrecked fortune, the loneliness, the bitterness, weighed on him more and more. He went to Paris, — seeking some facts about the life of Napoleon on which he was working. But the beauty of that gay capital could not bring back the old cheer and life and hopefulness to this breaking man. He went to Italy, the Government placing a ship at his disposal for the trip; but Italy, with its sunny skies, and wealth of art, could not bring into his veins the old tides of life which had run brimfull along Tweedside and Teviotdale. He came back to Abbotsford a wreck. The Esk and the Yarrow murmured, as he was borne along their banks, just as sweetly as they did fifty years before; but ear and heart and hopes were palsied.

Sometimes a gleam of the old life seemed to return, and he asked for his pens, his ink, and the old seat at his table.

Could he write? No, the weak fingers could not even grasp the pen. There was a new dog in the place of old Maida; he could pat *him*, and he did. He could say a kind word to this and that familiar friend; not saying all he would say, and stammering through the little he could say.

At last, in the sunshine on the Tweed banks, — there before his doors, — he summons Lockhart, his son-in-law, to his side.

"Will he have Anne (his daughter) called too?"

No, she — poor girl — has slept none the night past: he will not have her disturbed.

"Lockhart," he says, "be good — be virtuous; nothing else will bring you comfort when you come to the end."

It was the end — for this great Scotchman. A half-hour later, and he was wholly still.

If I had known all these things of him when our old master said, "Walter Scott is dead," — I should have felt very differently.

X.

ROBINSON CRUSOE.

Fifty Pounds Reward.

IN England, a great many years ago, — when Anne
had just become queen, and when the Duke of
Marlborough was making those dashing marches on the
Continent of Europe which went before the fearful and
the famous battle of Blenheim; and when the people of
Boston, in New England, were talking about printing
their first newspaper (but had not yet done it), — there
appeared in the *London Gazette* a proclamation, offering a reward of fifty pounds for the arrest of a " middle-
sized, spare man, about forty years old, of a brown
complexion, and dark brown-colored hair, who wears a
wig, and has a hooked nose, a sharp chin, and a large
mole near his mouth." And the proclamation further
said that " he was for many years a hose-factor in Freeman's yard, in Cornhill."

And what do you care about this man with a hooked
nose, for whose capture a reward was offered about the
year 1703 ?

Had he plotted to kill the queen? No. Had he forged a note? No. Had he murdered anybody? No. Was he a Frenchman in disguise? No.

What then?

He had written some very sharp political pamphlets, which the people in authority didn't at all like, and were determined to punish him for.

Daniel Defoe.

But I suppose there were a great many hot political writers who were caught up in the same way in those old-fashioned times, and put in the pillory or in prison for the very same sort of wrong-doing, whose names we don't know, and don't care to know.

Why, then, have I brought up this old proclamation about this forty-year-old, hook-nosed man?

Only because his name was Daniel Defoe, and be-cause he wrote that most delightful of all the story-books that ever were written, — ROBINSON CRUSOE!

To be sure, he had not written "Robinson Crusoe" at that time : if he had, perhaps the sheriff, or whoever sent out the proclamation, would have described him as the writer of a story-book about being cast away on a desert island, and full of monstrous fables, instead of describing him as a hosier of Freeman's Court. But I don't know. People in authority never know or care so much about the books a man writes, as about the shop he keeps and the debts he owes.

But did they catch the hook-nosed man? and did somebody get the fifty pounds?

Yes, they caught him ; and yes, too, — about the pounds.

Poor Defoe had not only to go to prison, but to stand in the pillory. Perhaps you do not know what the pil-lory was. It was a movable framework of wood, so arranged that a criminal was forced to stand in it with his head and hands thrust through holes in a plank ; and in this condition he was put on show in the public streets. It was an awkward position for a man to be placed in ; and when he was disliked by the crowd, he was pretty sure to have mud thrown at him, and to be met by jeers and hootings. What if some of our thieves and forgers were to be set up in this way at the head of Wall Street !

We thank God that we have outlived the times of such savage treatment. I wish we could thank God that we had outlived the crimes which seem to de-serve it.

But Defoe, in those political writings I spoke of, had said no worse things, and no more severe things, than we meet with nowadays in our newspapers. Nor was the crowd of street people imbittered against him : in fact, they brought garlands of flowers, and placed on the pillory, and threw roses in the street as the officers moved him from place to place.

He had been befriended by King William, who died only a short time before ; and who — as you know — had been brought over from Holland to govern England in place of James the Second, who had been driven away from the throne.

The Culprit's Work.

What had most brought him into favor with King William and his government, was a little pamphlet in rhyme which he had written, — called the True-born Englishman ; and this had met with great favor too, from the people of London. It had been written to show that those acted very unwisely who found fault with King William for being a foreigner, — and to show further that the whole population of England was made up by the mingling of different nationalities ; and that every man was to be judged by his devotion to the interests of Britain, and not by his race or birth. This would very naturally be well relished by a great city population, which had come from all quarters. No book — it was only a small pamphlet, to be sure — had met with so large a sale for years and years. Hence, I think, came those flowers which were hung upon the pillory where Daniel Defoe was set up in 1703.

He had written other things as well, which had made
him well known ;—among the rest a satire in rhyme
called, "Advice to the Ladies : Showing that as the
World goes, and is like to go, the best way is for them
to keep Unmarried."

You would think this a strange way to make himself
popular. But he says in the preface to this, — "You
will say 'tis a great fault to persuade People against
Marriage. I answer, 'That to the utmost of my power
I will ever expose those Infamous, Impertinent, Cow-
ardly, Censorious, Sauntering, Idle Wretches, called
Wits and Beaux, the Plague of the Nation, and the
Scandal of Mankind. But if Lesbia is sure she has
found a Man of Honor, Religion and Virtue, I will
never forbid the Banns : let her love him as much as
she pleases, and value him as an Angel, and be married
to-morrow if she will.'"

Now, as every young woman thinks she has found the
Angel, when it comes to the fact of marriage, I think
other flowers would have been given to Defoe on this
score.

But, nevertheless, he had the prison before him ; and
he tells us he had an awful time there, and chafed hor-
ribly. He was one of those restless, impatient busy-
bodies, who want always to be at work, and at work in
their own way. He did, in fact, edit a " Review " while
he was in prison, — and procured the printing of it, —
in which there was a great deal of sharp talk.

He was what would have been called in our time, I
dare say, a hot-headed radical ; and if he had been born
a century and a half later, would have made a capital
editorial writer for a slashing morning journal, in either

New York or Washington. But our people in authority would never have offered a reward for his arrest: they would have shrugged their shoulders; or, perhaps, have given him an office.

Yet, for all his political sharpness, this hook-nosed man had a head for business, — or, at least, for projects of business. Some four years before the prison experience, he had published an " Essay on Projects," which was full of excellent suggestions, but in advance of his time. Dr. Franklin relates, that he fell in with a copy of this book in his father's library, when a young man, and that he gained ideas from it, which had great influence with him in after-life.

The business project into which Defoe did really enter was the establishment of tile-works at Tilbury — where were made first in England those queer-shaped tiles for roofing, which — if you ever go there — you will see on a great many of the houses of Rotterdam and Amsterdam; and some of them are to be found yet upon old houses in some of our southern seaboard cities.

A few years ago — in 1860 — the workmen upon a new railway cutting dug through the meadow where these tile-works of Defoe had stood; and they turned up a great many broken tiles, and some curiously-shaped tobacco-pipes. And it happened that some visitor, who knew the history of the place, told these workmen that the tiles they were turning up had been made by the writer of Robinson Crusoe: straightway there was a rush to gather the best fragments — most of all the pipes. They had read the book.

I think I should have liked myself to lay hold of one

of those pipes, and compare it with one which Robinson contrived, and rejoiced over in his cavern, — though "it was a clumsy thing, and only burnt red like other earthern-ware."

But the prison life made an end of the pottery works. He could write in Newgate, and did; but he could not superintend the tile-yard.

There were good friends of his who meanwhile were bestirring themselves to loose poor Defoe from his prison life. Though he was doing more work there than most men were doing outside; yet the narrow bounds of the prison-yard, and the bad air, and the contact with all sorts of wretched criminals, were wearing upon his health and strength; so that when at last a messenger came to him from one high in power — asking what could be done for him; he says that he took his pen, and wrote the reply of the blind man in the Gospel, "Lord, dost thou see that I am blind, and yet ask what thou shalt do for me? My answer is plain in my misery, — Lord, that I may receive my sight."

This meant liberty; and he was given his liberty a short time afterward.

His Family.

I have told you he was the author of that book you all know so well; but because he wrote that book you must needs want to know who was his father, and what *he* did, and if he had a wife or children.

Well, his father was not a man who could put his son into relations with people in high place, — as Sir William Temple did for Jonathan Swift, — not far from the same time.

Defoe's father was a butcher — named James Foe — in the parish of St. Giles, in the city of London, — where Daniel was born. How his father's simple name of Foe grew into Defoe, is something that I am afraid could not be explained without saying that our good friend Daniel had the vanity to think that the long name sounded better than the short one ; — which is after all, no worse a vanity than that of our lady friend, who thinks a long ribbon to her hat is more becoming than a short one.

Not that Defoe was ashamed of his parentage : no, no, — ten times over. Always, when he speaks of his father, it is with respect and love. And there is nothing to show that he did not deserve it. He certainly sent him to a good school, and would have given him a training to be a clergyman ; this was not to Daniel's taste, so he became a hosier, and then — failing in that — went into tile-making (as we have seen), to which the prison brought an end.

A British admirer says that his grandfather, Daniel Foe, "kept hounds" in Northamptonshire, — as if keeping hounds to kill foxes (for sport) were a great deal better than keeping sharp knives to kill lambs (for food). Perhaps so ; at least it is one of those social puzzles with which the Daniel Defoe who wrote the True-born Englishman did not concern himself greatly. Hear what he says, in what is very bad poetry certainly : —

> " Then let us boast of Ancestors no more,
> Or Deeds of Heroes done in days of yore ;
> For Fame of Families is all a cheat :
> 'Tis Personal Virtue only makes us great."

But perhaps he wrote in this way because he could make no boast himself. It is poorly worth while to inquire. When we find a man writing common sense, the presumption ought to be that he writes thus because it *is* common sense.

Did the author of Robinson Crusoe have a wife and children? Oh, yes!—there were some six children, and a wife, to whom Queen Anne sent a gift of a hundred pounds—the while her husband was in prison. Defoe slipped out of London the moment he was set free from Newgate,—to go down and meet that wife and those children, who were living just then in the old town of Bury-St.-Edmunds.

[The name of that town sounds familiar: did you ever hear it before? Have you ever read Pickwick? Didn't Mr. Pickwick take a coach-ride in that direction once? And was there not an Angel Inn? and a man in a mulberry suit?]

He did not go back into trade,—either hosiery or tile-making; perhaps he saw his unfitness for it. There is something in a book he wrote called "The Complete Tradesman," which looks like it.

"A wit turned Tradesman!" he says: "what an incongruous part of Nature is thus brought together! No apron-strings will hold him; 'tis in vain to lock him in behind the counter, he's gone in a moment; instead of journal and ledger, he runs away to his Virgil and Horace."

But you must not believe he was very poor: some of the people about Queen Anne found out that he was a most serviceable writer; and he was sent down to Scotland, under pay, to help forward some designs of the government. The Scotch did not like him, for they did not like the business he was sent upon ; and though he wrote a poem on Caledonia to put them in good humor, it did not succeed.

His pen was all the while busy however, but mostly with political matter, which passed out of sight with the occasion that called it up. There was though an account of the apparition of Mrs. Veal (after death, and in

House where "Robinson Crusoe" was written.

a scoured silk gown) to one Mistress Bargrave, which set all the street world of London agog. It was so wonderfully told ! — so well told, people thought Mrs. Veal *must* have come to life ; and crowds went hunting after Mrs. Bargrave to hear if it were really so.

Fifteen years or more after he went out of prison, down to Bury-St.-Edmunds, we hear of him as living in a

big house which he had built at Stoke-Newington with a
coach-house attached. This meant — as it does not
always mean now — that he had money. There were
some five acres of pleasure ground attached, where he
pleased himself with working at gardening.

He had certainly three daughters living with him
there, besides his wife Susannah. And his daughters
were quick-witted, winning girls; Sophia being the
most so : she married, ten years later, a Mr. Baker, who
is authority for this account of them all.

And in this big, square, uncomely house, — of which
I show you a picture, — was written in the year 1718
by this hook-nosed man — then well on toward sixty
years of age — " The Life and Strange Surprising Adventures of Robinson Crusoe, of York, Mariner, who
lived Eight-and-Twenty Years, all alone, in an Unin-
habited Island on the Coast of America, near the mouth
of the great River Oroonoque."

The Book.

——— Ah, what a book it was ! what a book it is !

You do not even know the names of those political
pamphlets which this man wrote, and which made him a
friend of the great King William, and gave him fame ;
nor do you know the names of those others which
brought him to prison ; nor do you know the names of
those later ones which made Queen Anne befriend him,
and kept her his friend until the queen died ; nor do
you know — nor do your fathers or mothers know much
about those other books which this man wrote upon
Trade, and Religious Courtship, and a score of other

Robinson Crusoe.

things ; nor are they by anybody much read or called for. But as for that dear old figure — in the high goat-skin cap, — and with the umbrella to match, — and the long beard, — who does not know him, and all about him, all over the Christian world?

Why, long as it is since I first trembled over the sight of those savage footmarks in the sand, and slept in the cave, and pulled up the rope-ladder that hung down over the palisades, —yet, if that dear old Robinson in his tall cap and his goat-skin leggings were to march up my walk on some mild spring evening, I don't think I should treat him as a stranger in the least. I think I should go straight to him, and clap him on the back, and say, —

"My dear Mr. Crusoe, I'm ever so glad to see you!

"And did Friday come with you?

"And is Poll at the station?

"And have you been to York?

"And do you think of going to sea again?"

I don't know any figure of the last two centuries that it would be so hard to blot out of men's minds as the figure of Robinson Crusoe.

How came this hook-nosed man to write it?

Well — Queen Anne was dead : this had thrown him somewhat off his track. Then, the people about George I. who had just come to the throne did not much favor Mr. Defoe; perhaps they were afraid of him ; perhaps they thought him gone by, and useless. Perhaps Han-over George had too many friends of his own.

But what suggested such a subject? Was there really a Mr. Robinson whose father lived down at Hull?

No : but there had lived a man named Selkirk, —

Alexander Selkirk, — in Fife, Scotland, who went mate on a trading-voyage with Capt. Stradling, in a ship called the *Cinque Ports.*

Off the island of Juan Fernandez, which is abreast of Chili on the South American coast, Selkirk fell into a quarrel with his captain ; and, being a high-strung young fellow, he said he would rather be put ashore than to sail with the captain farther.

So the captain put him ashore — with only his bed-ding, a gun, and a very few such useful things. He staid alone on that island four years and four months before a British ship touched there by accident, and brought him off. He was in goat-skin clothes, and had his last shirt on when Capt. Dover took him off.

This much was all true as gospel, and was printed in Woodes Rogers's account of his voyage in 1712 (being seven years before Robinson Crusoe was printed) : the whole story of Woodes Rogers would have filled about one column of a newspaper.

Some jealous people said Defoe stole his story of Robinson Crusoe from it.

But a man can't steal a silver dinner-service out of a pewter plate.

He used the incidents without question, — as any one else might have done — but didn't. Ten shipwrecked men might tell their stories to you or me, and yet no Robinson Crusoe come of it.

There are plenty of good incidents all abroad ; it is the art which builds upon them that is rare, and which, in place of a jumble of words that will set the facts only before you, will twist out of them a drama that kindles your passions and your love, and dwells with you as a tender memory forever. And all this is done — not by fine words and long words, and by what young people are apt to call — splendid writing. This " splendid " writing is indeed a very bad thing to aim at, and the very last thing to admire. I wish all schoolmasters thought so ; but unfortunately they do not.

How could any thing be more homely and modest and straightforward than the language which Defoe uses to tell the adventures of Robinson ? Yet no words could be better for the purpose he had in mind ; — and that was — to make everybody feel that the things told of did really and truly happen.

There were critics, to be sure, who, in the day of its first printing, thought it was " carelessly written," and that there was a great deal which was very " improbable " in it ; and they didn't imagine for a moment that there was the stuff in it which would be pondered, and read over and over, and admired and dearly cherished — years and years after they and all their fair culture and fine words and very names should be forgotten.

I don't at all believe that Defoe himself knew how good a thing he had done. If he had, he wouldn't have gone about to weaken its effect by writing a sequel to Robinson ; which, though it has some curious and wonderful things in it, is yet hardly worth your reading. And not content with this, Defoe — under the spur, I suppose, of money-making publishers, — wrote, the next year, " Serious Reflections during the life of Robinson Crusoe, with his Vision of the Angelic World."

Nobody knows it or reads it. Poll and Man Friday are all alive ; but the Vision of the Angelic World is utterly dead.

Defoe also published shortly afterward the History of the Life and Adventures of Mr. Duncan Campbell; and in the same year Memoirs of a Cavalier. This last, however, was understood to be based upon a manuscript written by another hand. The following year there appeared by Defoe " The Life, Adventures, and Piracies of the famous Captain Singleton." But I cannot tell you, nor would you care to know, the names of all that he wrote. The titles alone, if I were to write them out in full, would fill a hundred pages as large as this.

His Religious Courtship may entertain you if you happen to be of age for thinking on such a subject; and his Complete Tradesman has a great many capital suggestions in it, — full of the pith which belonged to Poor Richard's maxims.

He wrote also a long history of the Great Plague in London, which is so dreadfully real that it would make you shudder to read it. You seem to see all the sick people, and the dead ones with their livid faces; and the wagons that bore the corpses go trundling every morning down the street. You would wonder, if you read it, how old man Defoe could have gone about prying amongst such fearful scenes, as if he loved grief and wailing and desolation ; for he don't tell you that he helped anybody, or even lifted the dead into the carts. How could he ? He wasn't there at all. The Great Plague raged and ended before Defoe was grown. He may have heard old men and old women talk of it; but he couldn't have been more than two years old when it first broke out.

Good-by, Robinson!

But I will close this half-hour's talk with only dear old Robinson Crusoe in our mind. Defoe wrote of him, as I said, when he was well toward sixty; and he lived to be over seventy, — having a great grief to bear at the last. His son deserted and deceived *him* as Robinson Crusoe had deserted and deceived *his* old father at York!

"This injustice and unkindness," writes Defoe to a near friend in the last year of his life, "has ruined my family, and has broken my heart. I depended on him, I trusted him, I gave up my two dear unprovided children into his hands; but he had no compassion, and suffered them and their poor dying mother to beg their bread at his door; himself, at the same time, living in a profusion of plenty. It is too much for me. My heart is too full. Stand by them when I am gone, and let them not be wronged."

This is a true letter of Defoe's, and one of the last which he ever wrote; but the old man was sadly broken in the latter years of his life, and looked too despairingly upon his home affairs: it is certain that his wife did not beg her bread, nor was she at that time in a dying condition. But I suspect there was only too good ground for his shaken confidence in the son; and I fear the poor old gentleman died without forgiving him, and without being asked to forgive.

He lies buried in Bunhill Fields — where Bunyan lies buried too. The epitaph which would commemorate him best would be one which should say simply, "He

wrote the story of Robinson Crusoe." And methinks
a figure of the dear old adventurer in his goat-skin
clothes, and his goat-skin cap, might well stand upon
his grave.

Saving Traps from the Wreck.

Who would not know it? Who has not read the
book? How could people help reading it? How could
they help being terribly concerned about the fate of

that madcap, who *would* leave that sober old father of
his in Hull, and that mother who cried over his fate,
you may be sure, more than ever you or I? Who could
help reading on, when he escaped so hardly from wreck
and death, on the shores of England, near to Yarmouth;
and fell in with such bad fellows in London; and hesitated, and wavered, and finally broke into new vaga-
bondage; and was followed up by storms and wreck,
and at last, as you know, cast ashore with scarce life in
him, on that far-away island, where he bewailed his fate
for months and years, and toiled hard, and tamed his
goats, and planted his palisades?

A great many thousand eyes looked out with him,
year after year, for the sail that never came. Of course
there had been a great many stories of adventures written before, and there have been a great many since;
but never, I think, any that took such hold of the feelings of all, as this story.

Why, do you know that crowds of people believed in
Robinson Crusoe when Defoe was living, and continued
to believe in him after Defoe was dead? I know I believed in him a long time myself; though the preface,
and the sober-sided old school-ma'am (who caught me
one day at the reading of it in school-hours, and made
me wear a girl's bonnet for punishment), — though such
as these, I say, warned me that it was a fable and
untrue, yet I kept on, somehow, believing in Robinson, and in Poll, and Man Friday; and thought, if I
ever *did* make a long voyage, and the ship *had* a yawl,
I would ask the captain, when he came opposite the
island, to "heave to," and let me go ashore in the yawl,
and find the cave and the creek, and very likely the

remnants of that big canoe in the forest, which Robinson Crusoe hewed from so huge a log—that he never could and never did move it.

Robinson at Home.

I believed in that old deserted father, down in Yorkshire:—somehow, I think he is living there yet,—repining, grieving, praying, weeping!

Oh, Robinson, Robinson!

XI.

HOW A TINKER WROTE A NOVEL.

Travels of Christian.

ONCE upon a time — years and years ago — I wanted some good Sunday book to read ; and when the want was made known, I was helped to a big, leather-bound, octavo book, which at first glance — notwithstanding one or two large splotches of gilt upon the back — did not look inviting. In the first place, what boy wants to grapple with a big octavo? Your precious old aunt will tell you what an octavo is, — that it means a book with its paper folded so as to make eight leaves of every sheet, whereas a duodecimo is one of paper folded so as to make twelve leaves to a sheet ; and this last is therefore much handier and every way better for boy use, — at least, I think so. Then it was bound in full calf — very suspiciously like a dictionary, and like — well, I must say it — like the Bible. I don't mean, of course, to breathe one word against that venerable volume ; but then, you know, when a fellow wants a good Sunday book, and knows just where the Bible is kept, and has read it ever so often, he doesn't want what looks too much like it.

However, there I was with the big book on my knee; and there were pictures in it. These were stunning. There was a picture of a man with a great pack on his back, doing his best to get out of a huge bog; and there were some people standing by, who didn't seem to help him much.

There was a picture of a prodigious giant, — fully as large as that in Jack and the Beanstalk story, — who was leading off two little men, — one of whom looked like the man that wore the big pack, and was near sinking in the bog. Then there was a splendid picture of this same little man walking up with all the pluck in the world, through a path, beside which were seated two old giants, who — judging from the bones which lay scattered around their seats — seemed to have been amusing themselves by eating up just such little men as the plucky one, who came marching up between them so bravely.

In short, the pictures carried the day; and though it seemed droll Sunday work, I wanted amazingly to find out how this plucky little man got through with his bogs and giants.

So I set to.

Christian was the man's name, and he had a family. But he became pretty well satisfied that he was living in a city that would certainly be destroyed; and was very much troubled about it, and couldn't sleep at night, nor let his family sleep.

So it happened that this Christian, after getting some directions from a man called Evangelist, "put out" one day, with his pack upon his back, and left his wife and children.

They did indeed run out after him so soon as they saw that he was fairly set off, and called to him very piteously and loudly, — which is not surprising, if he was a man of fair honesty ; but he — strangely enough, I think — put his fingers in his ears, and cried out, — "Life, life!" I didn't, in fact, at all like the manner in which the book makes him leave his family behind him. His course may have been well enough ; but why shouldn't he have taken them along with him, instead of leaving his children to be looked after by that fellow Great-Hear— But I mustn't tell the story in advance.

His going off in this way made a great deal of noise in the neighborhood ; and a Mr. Pliable, who was some-thing of a gossip, went out crossways to meet Christian, and have a chat with him, and was won over to keep by him, until they both tumbled into that great bog I spoke of. After floundering in this for a while, — Pliable abusing Christian for getting him in such a scrape, — they both crawled out. Pliable struck back, straight for home.

Christian kept on, — very wearily, with all that mire upon him in addition to his pack. A Mr. Worldly-Wise-man met him on the road. He was a pompous man, and had the air of knowing all that it was needful for anybody to know, and of having a well-filled purse besides.

When he heard that Christian was travelling to the Celestial City, he said, " Pooh, nonsense!" and advised him to go across to the town of Morality, where he himself had a snug house, which he sometimes occu pied. My impression is that he offered to rent it to him at a low rate. He told Christian, moreover, that Squire Legality, who lived there also, would take off his pack for him, — which, unlike most travellers, he was very anxious to be rid of : indeed, if he had valued it very highly, I think Mr. Legality would have taken it off all the same — if he had fallen in his way.

Christian does make a side-start on the Morality-road ; but Evangelist sees him before he has gone far, and puts him into the path he first chose. This takes him through a wicket, — where the keeper is very kind, — and brings him after a while to a place called the Interpreter's house, where he sees many wonderful things, — in visions, as it were. Among the rest, two boys named Patience and Passion, whom I haven't forgotten to this day. Patience took things very quietly, and had a good, honest, contented look ; — while Passion, with heaps of money, dashed it all abroad in a very reckless way.

He sees, too, here, — or thinks he sees (though it is hard to tell which of the two it is), a man shut up in a cage of despair, and who has a very sad time of it, beating against the bars of his den.

There was a house called Beautiful on his way, where he was received by two excellent persons, — Discretion and Charity. They took Christian to task, however, for having set off without his wife and family ; and his excuses were not of the best, I thought. However, they treated him well, and had him up in the morning to the top of the house, from which they pointed out to him the Delectable Mountains, that lay straight in his path. There couldn't be a finer country than that seemed to be, or than that proved to be, when he reached it at last. I don't think there was any thing in the book more enjoyable than that stoppage in the Delectable country; the very thought of it for years after brought up the loveliest images of fountains and sweetly-flowing streams, and vineyards, and the most luscious of fruits.

Passion and Patience.

I wondered why Christian did not stop there altogether. But it seemed to be a road whereon every one must travel — when once they had set foot upon it, — either in a wrong direction or a right one.

Vanity Fair was an extraordinary place he had to pass

through, with a sort of world's exhibition always going on in it, — with a French Row, and an Italian Row, and a British Row : I am sure there would have been an American Row if the author had known as much of our people as of the rest of Vanity Fair.

As for the city, it was not very unlike New York : the judges were worse, I think ; and Faithful, — who was the best of men (at least, he seemed so), gets executed there.

Christian made good speed out of it — so soon as he could.

I can't undertake to give the full order of his travel ; but I know he met a great monster, Apollyon, somewhere, a prodigious creature with scales, equal to any thing in the Arabian Nights. He strode wide across the way on which Christian was making his pilgrimage, and gave fight to him. My heart stood in my mouth at the first reading of this battle. Would Christian win ? It was "nip and tuck" with them for a long time, and I was not sure how it could come out. But at last Christian gave this Apollyon a good punch under the fifth rib, and the dragon flew away

There was a Giant Despair somewhere, who lived in Doubting Castle, in sight from the road. Christian was warned against him (I think he was in company with poor Faithful at this time), and they somehow strayed into his territory, and fell asleep.

This made one's heart beat. What if the giant should take a walk in their direction !

Why don't they wake up ? — we thought. But they slept, and slept. And the giant did come that way, and haled them into his underground dungeons. I think I gave Christian up at this pass.

This giant had a wife called Diffidence, — which seemed a very funny name for a woman who advised the giant — after they had gone to bed — to give Christian and Faithful a good sound beating every morning after breakfast.

He did give them a beating, and a good many of them ; and Christian would have been murdered outright if he had not bethought himself of a key he had — all the while — in his own bosom, and which would unlock any door in all Doubting Castle.

It was very stupid in him not to have thought of the key before ; but he didn't.

However, he used it at last, — unlocked the dungeon door, — helped up poor Faithful, — went along the stairs — very quietly, — tried another lock, — opened that (what if the giant should hear !), and it grated fearfully ; unlocked another and another, and at last they were safe outside once more, and made their way back to the true path which they had wandered from. They set up a column of some sort thereabout, — so that other people shouldn't get into the grounds of Doubting Castle again for want of warning. This was very good of them ; but I suspect it did not serve much purpose. Almost everybody stops to see Doubting Castle, and take the risk of being caught by Giant Despair.

Well, this plucky, earnest Christian went on, — meeting with hobgoblins, — worrying terribly in a certain Valley of Humiliation, — trembling as he walked between two great monsters called Pope and Pagan (he was foolish for that, — since these giants had their teeth drawn, or had worn off the sharp edges of them with long years of mumbling).

He enjoys himself hugely in the Delectable Moun-tains — (I was sure he would), and the hospitable shepherds entertain him very kindly: he reaches the

Escape from Doubting Castle.

worst in the valley of the waters of Death, but comes out all right at last by the shores of the river of Life, and passes on into the streets of the CELESTIAL CITY.

Great-Heart.

Don't forget that it was a Sunday on which I first read this book, and dreamed after it — of Apollyon (whom I imagined a monster bat, with wings ten feet long, and flapping them with a horrible, flesh-y sound) — also, of Giant Despair and his deep dungeon. (*If* Christian had happened to forget the key !)

I don't think I dreamed of old Worldly-Wiseman, or Pliable, or Legality, or Pick-thank. These are humble, riff-raff characters (to boys), compared with Apollyon. But the day will come when grown boys will reckon them worse monsters than even Apollyon, — by a great deal. I know I do.

There was a second part to this story, — though both parts were bound in one within the leather covers I told you of. It was too much together for one day's reading ; but I came to it all afterward.

The second part tells the story of Christian's wife and children. The good woman bewailed her husband, and bethought herself sorrily if she had been always to him what she should have been. She didn't for a moment accuse him for not taking her with him ; it appears now indeed — as if the author of the book had thought better of it — that poor Christian did urge and urge, over and over, that wife and children should together set off ; and that he did not put his fingers in his ears in that selfish way until all hope seemed gone.

Of course it had made much stir in their town, that Christian should have gone off in that manner ; and there were all kinds of rumors as to what had happened

to him, and many reports of his adventures; there were
those even who undertook to say where he actually was
at present, and what sort of robes he was wearing, &c.
As if they knew!

But Christiana — that was the name of Christian's
wife — did not cease to vex herself; and after much
thinking, determined to set off on the same journey her
good husband (she thought him good now that he was
gone) had taken the year (it may have been two years)
before.

When the packing began, and the news spread, you
may be sure there was a new stir in the town: the
gossips had a great feast in talking of it; and many of
them came to reason with Christiana, — and to see what
wardrobe she might be carrying; and to bid her an
affectionate good-by, and see what hat she might be
wearing on the journey.

One charming young person, whose name was Mercy,
and who was no gossip at all, and never knew how
many flounces anybody wore to their skirts, or what
they cost, — determined to go with Christiana. Christiana could not have had a better companion.

So they set off — children and all — this time. The
Slough of Despond (being the bog spoken of) was still
there, and in bad condition. The king of that country
had indeed given orders to mend this slough; and it
was said thousands of loads of waste material had been
dumped there, — for which the bills had been paid, —
still there was no sign of mending, and it continued as
grievous and plaguing as if it had been a highway of a
New-England town with the regularly elected select·
men puttering around it.

But Mercy guides them through safely ; and they go in high spirits through the first wicket, and reach in good time the Interpreter's house.

They see many things here — by reason, I suppose, of there being women of the party — which even Christian did not see ; amongst others, — a man raking everlastingly in a muck-heap, and never looking up. He was said to be a kind of stock-broker.

Great-Heart, the real hero of this second journey, takes them in charge to go on to the House Beautiful, and wards off a great many dangers from them on the way, — putting to death on the road a stout man by the name of Grim, who gave a great fright to Christiana's boys. Indeed, he showed such valor that the women entreated — Mercy especially — that he should keep by them altogether. He seems to have done so ; at least, he was always near when there was any fighting to be done.

There was a dapper little lawyer called Brisk, who introduced himself to the party at the House Beautiful, — he being a temporary boarder like themselves. He was a fine-spoken man, though a little airy. He greatly admired Mercy's housekeeping ways with her needle. He asks her how much she could earn at it ?

Aha, Lawyer Brisk ! But she wouldn't listen to his love-making ; and I was very glad when she said "No" to him.

If, indeed, it had been Great-Heart ! ———

One of Christiana's boys fell sick hereabouts with gripes, — from eating apples that fell from over the wall of Beelzebub's garden (I dare say Matthew shook them off himself). He is so poorly that they call in a Doctor

Skill, who has a large practice, and puts up pills which give the go-by very quickly to Beelzebub's apples.

As they go on, Great-Heart kindly shows the boys where their father Christian fought with Apollyon ; and he warns them all in the Valley of Humiliation to keep close by him. And it was extraordinary how the phantoms and monsters that threatened and growled, vanished when Great-Heart marched straight upon them without blinking. Lions, for instance, whose great feet the boys can hear pattering up over the grass after them in the dark, — when once they stand and face them, with Great-Heart close by, — turn, and are heard no more.

It's not so, however, with giant Maul : the fight with him was one of the hardest in the book. What a picture there was of it ! I would have liked to show you a copy of it ; but the printers who control these things say such pictures cost immensely, and wouldn't hear of it.

This Maul has a huge club, which he brandishes, and fetches Great-Heart a blow with it that brings that brave man to his knee. Mercy screamed, and thought it had been all up with him ; and so indeed did I, — at the first reading. But he gets upon his legs, and, after long parrying, gives Maul a thrust between his ribs that makes an end of him, and puts the boys and poor trembling Christiana in good case once more.

I forget now where, — but at one point they came up with old Honesty, — one of the very best fellows in all the book. It is so refreshing to meet with a new character ! The only thing I disliked about him was his putting in a favoring word when somebody hinted that

Mercy should marry Matthew, — the boy who was made sick with eating Beelzebub's apples. I never liked this. She was too fine a woman. Yet such young fellows somehow always get the fine women, and don't get — over eating Beelzebub's apples.

When the party came up to the stile that led over into the grounds of Doubting Castle, Great-Heart proposed to go over and call out giant Despair, and make an end of him.

At this point I remember my heart beat pit-a-pat again. Would he do it? Would the giant come out? Would Great-Heart have the better of him? What if the giant should throw a rock out of the windows upon him? Then there were nets in those grounds, and pitfalls; and Mrs. Diffidence with her hot water and spits.

However, Great-Heart did go; and did call him out; and did slay giant Despair, — as much as such a character can be slain. *That* Doubting Castle was pulled down then and there; but there has been a new one built, with modern improvements. The gentlemen who occupy it — philosophers among them — don't waylay strangers in the old manner: in fact, they give them strong, juicy meats to eat, and set them on the road again, in high spirits, — back to the town of Morality. There have been stories, however, that some of the younger dwellers in Doubting Castle, have, in a fit of passion, brained an innocent visitor or two, with some of the old bones lying about the premises.

They push on after this without very great adventures. They have a nice time at those dear Delectable Mountains, and through a spy-glass catch a glimpse of the Celestial City. Some think they see it, and some think they don't.

They don't mind the dangers of the Enchanted Ground much. Mistress Bubble with her fawning and fine jewels, and offer of *soirées* (I presume she gave amateur theatric shows), did not wheedle them at all.

They came to Beulah at last, and to the river brink, — and sang as they looked, —

> " Sweet fields beyond the swelling flood
> Stand dressed in living green."

Ah, but that Great-Heart was a noble fellow! Mercy ought to have married him; but it didn't end so. Great-Heart never married.

Well, that story in the leathern covers, and as big as a Bible, has been printed by hundreds of thousands, and has been translated into all the languages of Europe. And it was written by a travelling tinker. Think of that!

John Bunyan.

John Bunyan was his name; and he was born in a house built of timber and clay (which was standing not many years ago), in the little village of Elstow, near to Bedford, England.

Bedfordshire is a beautiful county: there are fine farms and great houses, and beautiful parks in it; but this man, John Bunyan, was the son of a travelling tinker, and was born there only a few years after the pilgrims landed from the Mayflower on Plymouth Rock. He says of himself that he was a wild lad, swearing dreadfully, going about with his father to tinker broken tea-pots, lying under hedges, having narrow escapes from death — once, falling into the river Ouse, and another time handling an adder, and pulling out his fangs with his fingers.

But he fell in with Puritan preachers, who "waked his conscience;" for he lived just in the heart of those times which are described in Walter Scott's novel of "Woodstock," and in that other novel of "Peveril of

John Bunyan

the Peak;" and he didn't think much of episcopacy or bishops; and at last he took to preaching himself, — having left off all his evil courses.

He married too, and had four children, — one of them, poor Mary Bunyan, blind from her birth. Bunyan loved this girl greatly. I think when he wrote of Mercy, — he thought of Mary Bunyan.

He fought in the civil wars under Cromwell, and it is
possible enough that he may have seen Charles the
First go out to execution. Maybe he was one of those
crazy fellows who came to Ditchley (in Scott's novel)
to help capture the runaway, Charles the Second, who
was gallivanting in that time in the household of old
Sir Arthur Lee. He throve while the Commonwealth

Bedford Jail.

lasted ; but when Charles the Second was called back
to the throne in 1660 (John Bunyan being then thirty-
two years old), it was a hard time for Puritans, and
worst of all for such Puritan of Puritans as the Puritan
preacher, — Bunyan.

They tried him for holding disorderly religious meet-
ings ; and he put a brave face on it, and contested his

right; but this only made the matter worse for him, and they condemned him to perpetual banishment. Somehow, this judgment was changed in such a way, that Bunyan, in place of being shipped to Holland or America (where he would have found a parish), was clapped into Bedford Jail, where he lay (he tells us) "twelve entire years." He had no book there but the Bible and Fox's Book of Martyrs. He made tag-lace to support his family, the while he was in jail, and bemoaned very much the possible fate of his poor blind daughter Mary.

While he was living his prison life, country people in England were reading the newly printed book by Isaac Walton, called the Complete Angler; and during the same period of time, John Milton published his Paradise Lost; and in that Bedford Jail, in those same years, John Bunyan wrote the story I have told you of, called the Pilgrim's Progress.

He came out of jail afterwards, — a good two hundred years ago to-day, — and took to preaching again. But he preached no sermon that was heard so widely, or ever will be, as his preachments in the Pilgrim's Progress.

He went on some errand of charity in his sixtieth year, and took a fever, and died in 1688. It was the very year in which the orthodox people of England had set on foot the revolution which turned out the Popish King James the Second, and brought in the Protestant William and Mary. Poor John Bunyan would have seen better times if he had lived in their day, and better yet if he had lived in ours, and written in the magazines as well as he wrote about Great-Heart.

Live as long as you may, you can never outlive the people that he set up in his story.

Messrs. Legality, and Cheat, and Love-lust, and Carnal-mind, we meet every day in society. Every boy and girl of you all will go by and by — slump — into some Slough of Despond ; and God help you, if the pack you carry into it is big ! Always, and at all times, there must be thwacking at dragons in our own valleys of humiliation ; and if the teeth of giant Pope are pulled, giant Despair — whatever Great-Heart may have done — will be sure to catch us some day in Doubting Castle, or somewhere else.

In fact, I don't much believe that Great-Heart did kill him ; and think — to that extent — the work is fictitious.

Giant Despair lives, you may be sure of it, — perhaps not in that same old Doubting Castle, which was probably pulled down. But he has a great many fine residences — in the city, and in the country too.

And he has a new wife ; and her name is not Diffidence now — oh, no ! but it is sometimes Dame Swagger, and sometimes Miss Spending, and sometimes Mrs. Dividends, and sometimes Lady Heartless.

As for that Valley of the Shadow of Death, — who that has lived since Bunyan died, or who that shall live henceforth, may escape its bewilderments and its terrors ? The poor tinker and preacher, — the zealous writer who made his words cleave like sharp knives, sleeps now quietly (to all seeming) in a grave on Bunhill Fields. And we shall have our resting-places marked out too, before many more crops of autumn leaves shall fall to the ground ; but evermore, the path to such resting-place, for such as he, and for such as we, must lie straight through the awful Valley of the Shadow of Death.

It would be a sad story if there were no Celestial City.

Bunyan's Tomb.